POINT CRIME

FADE TO BLACK

Stan Nicholls

SCHOLASTIC

To Marianne, the daughter I never knew I needed, with love.

Scholastic Children's Books
Commonwealth House, 1–19 New Oxford Street,
London WC1A 1NU, UK
a division of Scholastic Ltd
London ~ New York ~ Toronto ~ Sydney ~ Auckland

First published in the UK by Scholastic Ltd, 1997

ISBN 0 590 13774 3

Typeset by TW Typesetting, Midsomer Norton, Avon
Printed by Cox & Wyman Ltd, Reading, Berks.

10 9 8 7 6 5 4 3 2 1

Prologue

The orange that killed Silvester Whitbourne was grown in Seville.

That part of south-west Spain is always hot, and the groves thriving in its red, dusty soil bear fruit all year round.

Along with several hundred thousand others, the orange was hand-picked and boxed. Then the crates were taken by road to the Guadalquivir canal. There they were loaded on to boats for the next stage of their journey.

It was winter, and the streets of central London were bitterly cold, but Spain was the last thing on Silvester Whitbourne's mind. His only thoughts were of the brown paper package he clutched, and of getting back to Cornwall as quickly as possible.

Few of the people he passed, when they bothered

to notice him, supposed Whitbourne to be rich. They certainly had no reason to believe he was fabulously wealthy.

He was bundled against the weather in an ancient overcoat with a mismatched belt. His threadbare trousers were tucked into calf-high wool socks. One of his shoes, which had seen better days, had a broken, trailing lace. Locks of his unruly white hair poked out beneath a battered hat at least a size too small. The overall impression was of an elderly tramp.

Whitbourne was too preoccupied to notice the occasional glances he drew. And if he had known what the passers-by were thinking he wouldn't have cared. All he wanted was to be home, savouring his prize.

He hurried through the crowds towards the welcoming lights of the underground station.

When the orange that would end his life reached the Spanish coast, the crates were transferred to containers and put on a ship. It sailed on the evening tide and passed Portugal during the night. Dawn was breaking as it crossed the Bay of Biscay. By late afternoon of the following day the vessel had tied up at Southampton docks. Once there, the container with the box housing the lethal orange was lowered to a truck, which set out for a wholesaler.

After fumbling for change and buying a ticket,

Whitbourne rode an escalator down to the trains. It was warmer in the station but nearly as busy as the streets. He tightened his grip on the parcel and elbowed into the milling throng.

The far end of the platform was less crowded. He found a space and looked up at the destination board, confirming that the next train would take him to Paddington. Stamping his feet to rid them of the cold, his thoughts returned to the package.

He disliked London, with all its people, noise and traffic, and normally would have employed someone to bid for him at the auction he had just attended. But with such a precious item on offer Whitbourne felt he had to be at this particular sale in person.

Smiling, he cradled his find, glad that he'd made the effort.

At the wholesaler's warehouse the container was unloaded and the boxes put on to smaller trucks. The one carrying the orange in question headed north, making its delivery to the market in time for next morning's business.

At 5 a.m. a greengrocer bought the box, along with the rest of his needs. By 8.30 a.m., when his shop opened, the fruit and vegetables were priced and on display.

The first customer was a young woman who had recently started work as a secretary in the centre of town. She bought eight of the plump oranges to share in the office. After all, today was special. It was her birthday.

The carrier bag she came away with included the orange that would prove deadly to a man she had never met.

Whitbourne was growing impatient.

The destination board had listed his train as being due in four minutes for at least the last quarter of an hour. More people were filling the platform. Several had elbowed his package as they rudely shoved past him.

At this rate he wouldn't make his connection at Paddington, and the prospect of spending more time in London than was necessary began to depress him. He glared at his fellow travellers and silently cursed.

Someone bought a cake at lunchtime and the oranges were forgotten. After work, a group from the office invited the young secretary for a birthday drink. She rarely went into pubs, but she was new in the job and didn't want to seem unsociable. The bag of uneaten fruit went with her.

She intended to stay only long enough for one drink. Somehow this stretched to an hour and a half and three glasses of sparkling wine. The young secretary was unused to such a quantity of alcohol. Her head was swimming. When she realized it was time to go, she almost forgot the carrier bag.

She was unsteady on her feet as she made her way to the tube station.

The rails clicked and twanged. A distant rumble could be heard. Air rushed from the tunnel mouth. The train was coming at last.

Whitbourne moved nearer to the white line marking the edge of the platform. He stood on the words *MIND THE GAP* painted in fading yellow on the concrete floor.

The pressure of wind from the tunnel increased and the sound of the engine grew louder. People surged forward.

Among them was the secretary, still confused from the drinks as she battled against the jostling travellers. Someone barged into her. The paper carrier bag split, scattering bouncing fruit.

Whitbourne was unaware of this as the lights of the approaching train pierced the tunnel's inky blackness. The loco's thunderous roar echoed as it neared the platform. A blast of stale air buffeted him and he clasped the hat brim with his free hand.

Seven of the oranges dispersed in harmless directions.

The eighth rolled his way.

A tinny voice came on the public address system, but it was drowned by the train booming out of the tunnel. Whitbourne hugged his package.

The rolling orange arrived just as he was stepping closer to the edge.

His descending foot slipped on it. He lost his balance and tried to avoid dropping the parcel. It was a fatal decision. For a split second Silvester Whitbourne swayed uncertainly on the platform's edge.

Then toppled to the rails.

There was nothing the driver could do. He hit the brakes but the train was moving too fast.

It was over in an instant. There were shouts and gasps. Some of the onlookers screamed. Most averted their eyes.

Face white with shock, the secretary lifted a hand to her gaping mouth.

The orange was unharmed.

1

Heavy snow fell from a sky the colour of slate. The clapped-out minicab juddered as it hit another bone-rattling pothole. Ben bounced and thumped his head against the low ceiling. He sank deeper into the seat. The cheap plastic gave a squeak, but no relief from the rough ride.

He turned up his collar and shivered.

The driver was not a man given to smiling. A middle-aged, red-faced individual, he was barely visible beneath layers of jumpers and the windings of an absurdly long scarf. His hands, in gloves with the fingers and thumbs cut off, were clamped firmly to the steering wheel. He drove slowly, blinking into the blizzard beyond the windscreen. The lazy wipers were clogging with snow.

"Any chance of having the heater on?" Ben asked. His breath came in steamy huffs.

"Heater?" The driver let out a tiny snorting laugh. "Ain't got one. Never saw the need."

Ben was about to suggest that weather like this seemed reason enough when the driver added, "You're a Whitbourne, aren't you?"

"Is it that obvious?"

"I'd put money on it." He glanced at Ben's reflection in the rear-view mirror. The teenager's slightly moon-like face, prominent cheekbones, fine blond hair and soft blue eyes confirmed his opinion. "You've got the Whitbourne look, no doubt about that. And you're going to Adrian's Mount. Not much up there but the old boy's place."

"Yeah, Xanadu, my uncle Silvester's house. Did you know him?"

"Not really. Not to speak to, that is. Kept himself to himself mostly. But I saw him often enough to recognize the family resemblance. Shame about the accident."

Ben nodded, rubbing his palms together for warmth.

"Been here before?" the driver said.

"Not since I was a kid, and usually in the summer holidays. In recent years it's been … difficult for me to get here." He regarded the dismal landscape. "It all looks different to the way I remember."

"Cornwall can be quite a shock in winter if you've only seen it when the sun's shining. You here for the reading of the will, then?"

So much for keeping it in the family, Ben thought.

The driver read his passenger's expression. "News travels fast in a small community like this," he explained. "So they'll be others coming, will there?"

"Bound to be."

"They'll have to get a move on; this weather's only going to get worse. I reckon you were lucky the trains are still running." He ground the gears. The car bumped through a dip in the road covered by drifting snow. "You know, folk in these parts always thought your uncle Silvester was a bit..."

"Eccentric?"

"Yes. No offence, mind. But the first time I saw him outside that great house of his I thought he was the gardener. He certainly dressed for the part. And they say the place is like some kind of museum."

"My uncle spent his life collecting anything and everything to do with cinema. He *loved* films."

"Worked in 'em, did he?"

"No, he never did. I'm sure he would have dearly liked to, but his life was taken up with a whole load of other business interests. So he concentrated on making his house a kind of shrine to the movies."

"You know, your uncle lived here for years and I never knew that. But, as I say, he kept to himself."

"He was quite a private person in many ways. But I would have thought the name he gave to the house was a bit of a giveaway. You know, naming it after the castle in *Citizen Kane*."

The driver looked blank.

To Ben it was obvious. "Xanadu. From *Citizen*

Kane. It's the one of the most famous Hollywood movies ever. Orson Welles was in it. It was made in 1941 and—"

"Ah, black and white, is it? Might have seen it on telly. Prefer colour myself."

Ben realized they weren't going to pass the time discussing his favourite subject.

"Sounds like you're following in your uncle's footsteps," the driver remarked.

"Hm?"

"Films. Got the bug too, have you? Like him?"

"I suppose I have. As a matter a fact, I'm hoping to work in the industry." He smiled. "And I'm sure Uncle Silvester's responsible. He got me hooked on those visits in the school holidays."

Ben remembered how much he enjoyed his stays at Xanadu. The house was a treasure trove of movie memorabilia, and Silvester was the perfect host. He proudly displayed props and models, ran movies in his private cinema and recommended books on film making. His patience with his young nephew was infinite, and he was always kind. Ben was sad to think he'd never see him again.

His memories were interrupted by the driver announcing, "We're not far off now."

The road began to climb. To the left, Ben could just make out the sea. It was dark, with angry waves whipped by the wind. To the right rose the sheer cliffs of Adrian's Mount. The snow became more intense the higher they went. They dropped speed as the route narrowed and twisted.

By the time the road levelled they were edging along at walking pace. On such a high, exposed place the snow storm held full sway. It was hard to make out anything ahead of them. But eventually the driver managed to find the side road leading to the Mount's highest point, where Silvester Whitbourne's house stood.

Solid shapes appeared in the dazzling whiteness. As they drew closer, Ben realized they were the pillars on either side of the house's gates. In front of each pillar stood a large bronzed statue. Ben had forgotten about them. Seeing them again, their heads and shoulders laden with snow, he had to grin at his uncle's sense of humour. The statues were of the Academy Award, twin Oscars standing guard at the entrance.

They rode through the open gateway and along the drive. The estate's grounds were extensive and the path took several turns before a huge dark silhouette came into view.

Xanadu.

There was a break in the flurry of snow, allowing Ben his first sight for years of the rambling manor house. It was as big and sprawling as he recalled, and just as dramatic. And it shared something with its late owner. Like Silvester, the house was best described as eccentric. Wings and extensions added over the years had given it a jumbled, makeshift look. Everything seemed to be oddly out of true, with hardly a straight line to be seen. There were two towers, one at the end of the building, imposingly tall; the other, shorter, jutted from roughly the centre. They added to its strangeness.

Xanadu somehow appeared unreal. It reminded him of a film set.

Ben had another impression, one he had never felt during his happy childhood visits. The house he remembered with such affection now seemed sinister. It was shadowy and grim. Only one or two lights were on and it looked spooky against the weakly setting sun. Maybe it was the gloomy weather, or the fact that he was here because of a death.

Whatever the reason, it was natural for Ben to think in movie terms, and the ones he thought of at that moment were horror movies. He recollected the houses in *Psycho* and *The Amityville Horror.* His imagination conjured images of *The House on Haunted Hill* and Dr Frankenstein's and Dracula's castles. A thousand scenes from a thousand screen chillers filled his mind.

But he wasn't the sort of person who went in for flights of fancy. He let films do that for him, in darkened cinemas or on the smaller screen when he watched videos at home. So he did his best to shake off the ominous feeling the house gave him.

The minicab had drawn up opposite the front door. As Ben paid, the driver said, "I won't hang about. I don't want to get stuck up here in this filthy weather."

Ben got no help unloading his suitcase. As soon as he had, the minicab pulled away and quickly vanished into the stinging snow.

He was numbed by the cold, and once the car was out of earshot, the silence was total. Lifting the case, he crunched over to the door. It was solid oak and massive, with a Victorian bell-pull to one side. He tugged at it. A tinkling chime sounded somewhere deep in the heart of the house.

Nothing happened for a full minute. Then the door slowly creaked open.

A dim light in the hall showed a woman in sombre dress; dark blouse, full-length black skirt and flat, sensible shoes. The whiteness of her face seemed as much due to a pallid complexion as make-up. Tall, and probably in her fifties, she held herself stiffly.

The look she gave him was no warmer than the weather.

Ben thought of horror movies again.

2

The woman's nostrils flared as though she'd detected a bad smell. She regarded him sternly and snapped, *"Yes?"*

"Er, hi. I'm Ben Whitbourne." He got no response and added, "I'm here for the reading of my uncle's will."

"I didn't imagine it was a social call," she replied curtly. She had a thick foreign accent, possibly Eastern European, but Ben couldn't identify it. Moving aside, she said, "I suppose you'd better come in. And wipe your feet." She pronounced it *vipe*.

He obeyed the command while she closed the door.

"Leave your case," she ordered. "I'll have it taken to your room. You can hang your coat on the peg."

Ben felt her watching him as he did so. He tried to break the ice. "This weather's pretty awful, isn't it?"

"It's beyond our control so there's no point in discussing it."

Not keen on chit-chat then, he reflected wryly as he followed her into the house proper.

"I am Miss Olga Stanislavovich," the woman informed him grandly, "your late uncle's housekeeper. I do not believe I have seen you before."

"No. I haven't been here for—"

"Quite," she interrupted. "Very few members of your uncle's family have been to this house in recent years. No doubt they will find the time today, however, to hear his will."

Ben felt offended at the implied insult.

"You are, of course, welcome," she carried on, sounding far from welcoming. "But I should tell you that Mr Silvester lived quietly and liked an orderly routine. I see no reason why his death should change that. You'll oblige me by being punctual for meals and respecting your uncle's property. A disciplined house is a happy house."

Happy? Ben thought. *Good grief, the woman's a stormtrooper!* But he simply nodded agreement.

"Where are your parents?" she asked abruptly.

The question verged on rudeness. He bit back the urge to tell her to mind her own business. "Dad's in Hamburg, my mother's in the States. I'm sort of representing our branch of the family."

"I see." Her tone was brittle. "A big responsibility for one so young."

He resented that too, but didn't rise to the bait.

"You are the first to arrive," Miss Stanislavovich told him, "apart from your uncle's lawyer, Mr

Dominic Parker. He wants to greet each of you personally, so I will let him know you are here. Please wait." She turned and glided away. Ben was relieved to be rid of her. She gave him the creeps.

Standing alone in the main entrance hall, his memories flooded back. There was evidence of Uncle Silvester's obsession with films on all sides. Framed stills and movie posters lined the wall. Several glass cases displayed prized items. One housed a collection of revolvers from various westerns. Another held costume jewellery. The largest cabinet contained a ball gown once worn by Marilyn Monroe.

But what dominated the ground floor was the magnificent staircase, which Ben suspected was one reason his uncle decided to buy the house. It looked as if it had been transported from an old Hollywood musical. He wouldn't be surprised to see Fred Astaire and Ginger Rogers tap dancing down the marble steps.

At that moment, Ben was struck by the same uneasy feeling he'd had when he stood outside, and thought again how much the place looked like a movie set. An empty set, waiting for a drama to unfold.

In his mind's eye, Fred and Ginger became Freddy Krueger and Boris Karloff. Shadowy corners of the ill-lit hall suddenly seemed ominous. The measured tick of the grandfather clock began to sound threatening.

He was back to horror movies.

It occurred to him that Olga what's-her-name could be straight out of one. The homicidal housekeeper with an axe who—

"Mr Whitbourne?"

His heart skipped a beat. He spun around. She was standing behind him, face as sour as a fresh lemon. Ben gave a meek smile to disguise his embarrassment.

"He will see you now," she said. "In the study."

She insisted on escorting him. On the other side of the study door, Parker sat hunched at a large mahogany desk. He was in his late sixties or early seventies, his clothing conservative and dull. Strong bifocals, clamped to a hawkish nose, magnified his black pinprick eyes. His expression was humourless and slightly hostile. He didn't get up. *Another joyful soul*, Ben decided.

Miss Stanislavovich made the briefest of introductions. Parker nodded distractedly and waved Ben into the only other seat. The housekeeper hovered for a moment before noting the lawyer's glare. Then she silently left the room.

Parker was writing something. "One moment," he requested without looking up, his voice as arid as Ben expected it to be.

He glanced around as he waited. One wall of the study was entirely covered with mounted photographs of film stars. All were autographed, many with personal messages to Uncle Silvester. Models, magazines, books and other small objects of movie memorabilia occupied most of the shelves. They were even stacked on the floor in places.

Parker replaced the cap of his fountain pen. Then he cleared his throat, the way lawyers do, to gain Ben's attention.

"Let me see," he muttered, consulting a stack of papers, "you are Benjamin Whitbourne, my late client's nephew."

"That's right."

"And your parents are not able to be here?"

"No. They're both abroad."

"And divorced, I believe."

"As it happens, yes." Ben resented the intrusion into his private affairs. But he decided to head off any further questions on the subject by adding, "Things aren't that good between them at the moment and they weren't keen on being here together. So it was decided I should come."

The lawyer peered at him over his glasses. It was the look of someone who obviously found dealing with a teenager beneath him. "Did you ever meet Silvester Whitbourne?" he enquired.

"Oh, yes. Not during the past few years because of my parents splitting up. They both tend to work overseas and I've spent a certain amount of time with one or the other of them. Not to mention school and college making it difficult. But I often came here for holidays as a child." He paused. "I was very sorry to hear about Uncle Silvester's accident. I liked him."

"Quite so." The response was brisk and dismissive.

He doesn't seem exactly devastated by the loss, Ben thought. *But then, why should he? He's here on business, after all.*

"Your uncle's instructions," the lawyer explained, "are to reveal the contents of his will this evening after dinner. Providing the other relatives have arrived by then, that is, which in view of this quite exceptional weather is far from certain."

"Can you tell me what the will says?"

The look of disapproval came again. "I'm afraid not. That would be quite unethical until all members of the family are present."

"I'm just concerned about my uncle's collection," Ben assured him. "I'd like to see it preserved. And I know he would have felt the same way."

"You will have to be patient for a few more hours in order to learn your uncle's wishes." It was a put-down, delivered to what Parker no doubt considered an uppity kid. "I can tell you, however, that your uncle's estate is substantial. Although a great deal of his fortune is tied up in the ... *collection*." He made the word sound vaguely obscene.

"You don't seem too enthusiastic about his life's work."

"It's not for *me* to comment on the way my clients choose to spend their money," Parker replied indignantly. "But had he listened to my advice he could have invested it more conventionally."

"Perhaps not more wisely, though," Ben suggested. "I mean, the collection's unique. Its potential value must be enormous. And I bet he had a lot more fun building it up than he would have had playing with boring stocks and shares."

Parker frowned. Fun was a word that clearly didn't feature in his vocabulary. The muffled sound of the doorbell reached them.

"That will be the doorbell," the lawyer commented unnecessarily.

They sat in awkward silence, aware of movement and indistinct voices outside. Shortly, there was a knock on the study door and Olga came in. "It's another one of ... *them*, Mr Parker," she sniffed.

"Thank you, Miss Stanislavovich. I'll be ready in just a moment."

She *hurrumphed* and went away, mumbling about the upheaval to her routine.

"Until later then," Parker said, pointedly.

Ben knew a dismissal when he heard one. Closing the study door quietly behind him, he scanned the hall. It was deserted, so he went into the sitting-room. The only light came from a couple of table lamps and a log fire in the enormous hearth. In common with the rest of the house, the room was packed with the fruits of Silvester's years of collecting. But they couldn't be seen in detail because of the soft lighting. Anyway, Ben was more interested in warming himself.

A pair of armchairs faced the fireplace. He was level with them before he realized somebody was slumped in one.

3

She seemed to be asleep.

Ben had never seen her before, but he knew instantly that she was a Whitbourne. She had *the look* the minicab driver referred to. The rounded face and slightly protruding cheekbones; the sandy blonde hair, in her case shoulder length. He was sure her eyes would be mild blue, like his own and the other Whitbournes he'd met.

She was about his age. Dressed for travelling, in jeans and a chunky green sweater, she'd kicked off high, sturdy leather boots to warm her feet at the fire. Her breathing was deep and regular.

As he started to creep away she woke up.

The young woman stretched and yawned. She gave him a broad, easy smile, not in the least put out at finding him there. He was right about her eyes.

"Hello," he said softly. "Sorry I disturbed you."

"Hello yourself," she replied, shifting in the armchair. "Excuse me, I must have dozed off. It was a long journey." She yawned again, a hand over her mouth. "Anyway, I'm glad it was you."

He didn't understand, and it showed.

"Rather than the Bride of Frankenstein again," she explained.

Ben grinned at the unflattering but rather appropriate description of Olga. "She is a bit of a scream queen," he agreed. "My name's Ben Whitbourne."

"Then you and I are distant cousins. I'm Lorna Ferguson."

He remembered hearing about her, but didn't recall them ever meeting. "Hi, Lorna." He took her outstretched hand. It was soft, but the grip was firm.

"Now let me think," she said, "I know a bit about our family. Your parents are ... Dean and ... Penny?"

"That's right."

"Are they here?"

He explained why they weren't and she gave him a sympathetic smile. Then he asked after hers.

"I'm an orphan as a matter of fact. Have been for nearly five years."

"That's a tough break. Come to think of it, I remember my parents going to the..." He trailed off awkwardly.

"To the funeral. Don't worry, it doesn't upset me to talk about it."

It started to come back to him. "There was an accident of some kind, wasn't there?"

"Car crash. When they were on Malta. I wasn't there."

"Sorry."

"Don't be. I'm over it now."

She glanced at one of the windows. Snow cascaded on the other side of the glass. "This weather's ridiculous, isn't it?"

"Yeah. How did you get here, incidentally?"

"Same way I get just about everywhere: by motorbike."

That explains the boots, Ben realized.

"Nearly didn't make it though," Lorna continued. "These conditions aren't good for bikes. Had to push it up most of that blasted hill."

"Where have you come from?"

"Manchester. I'm at university there."

"This your first time at Xanadu?"

"Yeah, and I've been looking forward to seeing it for years. Oh, that sounds awful, doesn't it? Considering why we're here."

"No, I know what you mean." He told her how much he enjoyed visiting as a child.

"You lucky beggar!" she exclaimed with mock envy. "I would have *loved* coming to an amazing place like this when I was a kid. But we spent most of our time abroad."

"We've got that in common. I enjoyed travelling with one or other of my parents, but the downside was not getting to see Uncle Silvester or this house. You like movies, then?"

"Adore would be a better word. How about you?"

"Nuts about them." He smiled, delighted that she shared his passion. "In fact, my ambition's to work in the business. And that's down to our uncle's influence."

"With me, cinema was an escape after my parents died. It helped me get over the trauma. I sort of lost myself in films, and that led to an interest in how they were put together. What job are you hoping to do?"

"Special effects. I've done some amateur work, on video mostly, and I've got a place at a London film school, starting next summer."

"Wow, I'm impressed. Me, I'd like to *write* about films rather than make them. My ambition's to get into journalism and specialize in movies."

"Brilliant. It's a pity you never met our uncle, you would have liked him."

"Yeah, it's a shame. He sent money, you know. To help out when I was orphaned. Even though we'd never met, as far I'm aware. I appreciated that."

"It's the sort of thing he would have done. He was one of the good guys."

"'He wore a white hat,'" she quoted, "as they used to describe the heroes in old cowboy movies." Then her expression grew sombre. "The way he died was pretty gruesome, wasn't it, Ben? Under the wheels of a train like that..." She shuddered.

"They said it was over quickly."

"Who did?"

"The police. I went to see them before leaving town. They gave me the details."

"What was Silvester doing in London? Wasn't he supposed to be some kind of recluse?"

"Not entirely. He just preferred Cornwall, and this house in particular, to anywhere else. He was in London for an auction of movie material. There was something special he wanted. He got it, too."

"What?"

"The storyboards from *The Wizard of Oz*. You know what storyboards are, of course?"

"Course. Like I said, I'm into movies too. They're kind of strip cartoons of a film the studio gets an artist to draw before going into production."

"Then you'll know some can be incredibly rare because there's only the one set. For a classic like *Oz* they must have cost Silvester a small fortune. The ironic thing is that if he hadn't tried protecting them he might not have fallen in front of the train."

"That's a really tragic story."

"Yeah. But without being callous, I like to think it was the way he would have wanted to go."

Lorna's gaze swept the rapidly darkening room and the portion of Silvester's collection it contained. "Plus he did have a lifetime gathering all this together, which must have given him a lot of pleasure. And from what little I've seen of the collection so far, and all I've heard about it, it must be worth … well, *millions*."

"It probably is," Ben confirmed. "What worries

me is that whoever Silvester's left it to could be tempted to sell it off. I'd hate to see that."

"So would I."

He was glad she agreed with him. It felt like he had an ally.

The doorbell rang. They saw Olga silently passing the half open sitting-room door to answer it.

"Hopefully that's somebody human," Lorna joked.

Stifling giggles, they tiptoed over to peek at the new arrivals. Two men and a woman, all middle-aged, had dumped their luggage. They were shaking out snowy overcoats and hats, and grumbling about the weather.

"Recognize any of them?" Ben whispered.

"Only vaguely. But I might have heard gossip about them. I'll fill you in after we've been introduced. Which should be any minute now, so let's not get caught like a couple of kids eavesdropping."

They went back to the fire. Ben clicked on a standard lamp, then leaned against the mantelpiece, trying to look casual. Lorna began pulling on her boots.

The latest guests came into the sitting-room. Both men were evidently Whitbournes. It was the woman, however, who opened the conversation.

"Good afternoon," she said, coolly eyeing Lorna and Ben. "I'm Belinda Whitbourne. And you are...?"

"Ben Whitbourne."

"Lorna Ferguson. Hi."

Belinda, dark haired, hatchet-faced and dressed in an expensive but drab navy blue two-piece with pearls, grabbed the arm of one of the men. He wore a grey suit and black horn-rimmed glasses. There was something ferret-like about him. She dragged him forward.

"This is my husband, Jeremy. He's your uncle ... or something." She already seemed to be losing interest in them.

Jeremy's greeting was so gently spoken Ben didn't hear most of it.

There was a clumsy silence as Lorna and Ben waited to be told who the other man was. By far the tallest person in the room, he was lean to the point of skinniness. His sports jacket, slacks and loafers were smart casual. He was sun-tanned and had a pencil-thin moustache.

As Belinda seemed to be doing her best to pretend he wasn't there, he stepped forward to introduce himself. "I'm Rufus Whitbourne, another of your uncles." He beamed and stuck out his hand. "Happened to meet good old Jeremy and Belinda outside the station. I couldn't get a taxi and they were kind enough to offer me a lift."

"It's not as though you gave us much choice," Belinda muttered darkly.

Rufus ignored the gibe. He made for a drinks cabinet in the corner of the room. Sorting through the bottles, he called, "Anyone care to join me?"

Ben and Lorna chorused, "No, thanks."

Belinda was poker-faced. "I *don't*," she frostily informed him.

Jeremy brightened. "I think I might manage a small—"

"He won't have one either," interrupted Belinda.

Her husband's face dropped.

Rufus had already downed his first drink and was pouring a second by the time the others seated themselves. He continued loitering at the cabinet.

An awkward silence descended again.

Jeremy attempted some small talk. "Awful weather, isn't it? We were saying on the way down—"

"That it seems unnatural," Belinda finished for him. "It's this global warming they keep going on about. What did I say, Jeremy?"

"You said—"

"I said it's only to be expected with all those scientists tinkering around with things they don't understand. Isn't that right, Jeremy?"

"Yes, dear." He gave her a docile smile.

Ben glanced at Lorna. She raised an eyebrow, ever so slightly, and he had to look away to prevent himself laughing.

"Are you the first to arrive?" Jeremy asked them. Ben was surprised he completed the sentence without Belinda's help.

She supplied the answer, though. "You know they were, Jeremy. That … *foreign woman* told us so. Don't you ever listen?"

Jeremy went back to being meek and didn't

respond.

"It looked like there was another car on the road some way behind us," Rufus offered. "Could be more of the clan." He drained his glass and worked on a refill.

Jeremy tried again. "We were very sorry to hear about—"

"Silvester's accident," Belinda interjected, cutting him off once more. "Most regrettable."

Everyone nodded solemnly.

"I think a toast would be in order," Rufus decided. "Anyone?" There was a general shaking of heads. "Oh, well." He raised the glass. "Here's to Silvester. May he rest in peace." He took a gulp and smacked his lips.

Belinda leaned over and ran her finger along the edge of a bookshelf. "Um. I wonder who cleans the place? The way all this bric-à-brac attracts dust, it must be a full-time job."

"You sound as though you don't approve of Uncle Silvester's collection, er, Aunt Belinda," Ben said.

She didn't look too pleased with the *aunt* bit. "I'll say I'm not. A grown man, spending good money to accumulate this ... *trash*. But Silvester was always an odd type and one grew to expect that kind of nonsense from him. Don't you agree?"

Ben was about to tell her he certainly didn't.

Then there was somebody else at the door. *Saved by the bell*, he thought.

4

A few minutes later two more Whitbournes entered.

One was in his late thirties, the other maybe a decade less. Both wore stylish, designer brand suits. The older man sported a dark green velvet waistcoat under his jacket. He differed from the family norm in having black hair, which Ben assumed had been dyed. The younger man's was Whitbourne blond, cut short and slightly spiky.

They oozed wealth.

And were too busy squabbling to notice they weren't alone.

"I *said* we should have brought the Range Rover and not the BMW," the older man grumbled.

"OK, OK, you've made your point. Now give me a break."

"Well, if you hadn't –"

Belinda cleared her throat with an attention-grabbing *uhp-uuhm* noise. They stopped bickering, apparently aware of the others for the first time.

"Ah," the older one said, "some fellow members of the tribe. I'm Felix Whitbourne." He jabbed a thumb at his companion. "This is my kid brother, Crispin."

Crispin greeted them with "Ciao."

Ben noticed a flash of red braces beneath his open jacket. *Just what we need*, he thought, *a couple of ageing yuppies*.

Introductions were made. When the brothers reached Ben and Lorna her knowledge of family relationships proved helpful again. "We're your cousins," she explained, "twice removed, I think."

"Yah," Felix responded, without a trace of interest. He consulted his platinum Rolex. "Any idea when the will's being read? We're on a tight schedule."

"After dinner," Ben told him. "I gather you'll get to see Uncle Silvester's lawyer, Mr Parker, before that and—"

"*Damn*," Felix cut in. He turned his back on Ben and addressed his brother. "Looks like we'll have to spend the night in this dump."

"Typical Silvester," Crispin scoffed, "first he pops his clogs without warning, then we have to waste time hanging around his mausoleum of a house."

Neither of them seemed aware of the shocked hush they'd brought to the room.

Ben decided he wasn't going to get on with his new-found cousins. From the look on Lorna's face she felt the same way.

Rufus asked if the brothers wanted a drink.

Crispin refused with a vague shake of his head.

"Nor me," Felix said. "I need to keep alert, know what I mean?"

"The whole bloody family seems to be on the wagon," Rufus muttered, raising his glass.

Nobody paid him any attention.

"I'd better let the office know what's happening," Felix announced, "and get them to redirect my calls here." He snapped his fingers at Crispin. "Give me the mobile."

Crispin patted his pockets, then looked sheepish. "I, er … I must have left it in the car."

"You fool!" Felix sneered. "I can't trust you with the simplest job, can I?"

The doorbell chimed yet again.

"That thing's starting to sound like a wretched alarm clock," Rufus commented. He was growing a little slurred.

Felix and Crispin carried on sniping at each other. Ben tuned out their quarrel and tried to catch the new voices in the hall. There were several, none distinct, but one dominated the rest. It was loud, brash and American.

Belinda caught it too. Her caustic expression etched itself deeper.

A large, assured-looking man strode into the sitting-room. His broad smile showed impossibly white teeth. He was near totally bald, such hair as he had being silver, the colour probably out of a bottle labelled *Distinguished*. His tan was yellowish-orange.

He was dressed so loudly it was almost painful to look at him. A sky-blue suit clashed with his pink shirt and brown suede shoes. There was a chunky gold bracelet around each of his wrists. His tie was what you'd expect to result from an explosion in a paint factory.

Even Felix and Crispin noticed him, and piped down.

"Hi, folks!" the American boomed. "I'm Tyrone Milhouse."

As the gathering murmured their welcome a woman came through the door. She was all frilly peach dress and big hair. Her dazzling smile and not quite natural tan matched his. At least as old as Belinda, she was considerably better preserved.

"This is Gwendoline, my wife," Milhouse told them.

"Hello," she beamed, then started to circulate, clasping hands and pecking at cheeks. Belinda suffered her kiss through a frozen expression.

Lorna stretched over to Ben and said under her breath, "Gwendoline is Silvester's sister. Our aunt."

"Drink, old boy?" Rufus asked Milhouse.

"You bet. Mine's a bourbon. Boy, I just love your Brit hospitality!"

Ben winced.

"Like a drink, honey?" Milhouse called to his wife.

"Sure, Ty. Only I was wondering where that baby of ours has got to."

"Yeah. *Sweetheart!*" he roared at the door. "Get in here and meet the family!"

The person who appeared didn't so much come into the room as make an entrance.

"And here's my little girl," he declared. "Helena Belle Milhouse!"

His "little girl" was roughly Ben and Lorna's age. If she had a tan it was well covered by thick layers of make-up. Her permed curly locks were decorated with an outsized bow of the same material as her black full-length cocktail dress. It was sequinned. So were her stockings. She had on what could have been tap-dancer's pumps.

Helena Belle spread wide her arms as though ready to receive their applause. Her head tilted to one side in what she seemed to imagine was an appealing, cute kind of way.

"Hello, everybody!" she lisped.

Ben's jaw dropped. He turned to Lorna and whispered, "*What in hell's name is* that?"

Their ribs hurt from laughing so much.

"It was touch and go whether I could keep a straight face," Ben admitted.

"Me too," Lorna confessed, still breathless. "For one terrible moment I thought she was going to *sing*!"

They were in his room, having escaped the zoo

downstairs. Shortly after the Helena incident, which had even Belinda biting her lip, Olga came to say Parker was ready to see everyone. Lorna was first. As soon as it was over she and Ben made an excuse and got away.

Ben's room, in common with most of the others at Xanadu, had a movie theme. It was based on historical epics.

Among many other things, there were framed posters for *The Vikings*, *El Cid* and *The Three Musketeers*. Photographs of Douglas Fairbanks, Errol Flynn and Kevin Costner from different versions of *Robin Hood* also adorned the walls. A broadsword, a crossbow and a pair of daggers, all used as props in movies, were displayed in a glass case. One corner was dominated by an impressive suit of armour from a film about King Arthur.

They sat facing a large window, watching the falling snow outside.

"OK," Ben said, pulling himself together, "now tell me what you know about our relatives."

She dabbed her eyes with a tissue. "Well, one or two I probably met when I was a kid, but what I know about them comes mostly from my parents. They were fascinated by the family's antics. My dad in particular. He was even playing with the idea of writing some kind of family history when he and Mum..." Her face darkened, just for a second. But before Ben could say anything she shook off the sadness and added, "Where shall I start?"

"It has to be with Helena."

"Right. She reminds me of something a famous American journalist called Walter Winchell once said: 'Hollywood shoots too many pictures and not enough actors.'"

Ben giggled. "I like it!"

"Not that she can be called an actor by any stretch of the imagination," she added. "She's a Hollywood brat who's convinced she's going to be a star, and behaves like one. Trouble is, she's got no talent. For years she's been going to expensive acting schools, dancing and deportment classes, you name it."

"Doesn't seem to have done her much good. Tell me about her parents."

"Tyrone Milhouse is a film producer."

Ben snapped his fingers. "*Chainsaw Ghouls Ate My Driving Instructor!*"

"I *beg* your pardon?"

He grinned. "It was one of his pictures; a spoof horror movie. Did quite well a few years back. Thought his name rang a bell. I had no idea we had any actual film people in the family, though."

"I'm surprised you didn't know he was in the clan, given your interest in movies."

"All I heard was that Aunt Gwen had married an American, but that happened after I lost touch with Silvester."

"Tyrone had several box office hits, didn't he?"

"Yeah, but like I said, that was several years ago. And in Tinseltown you're only as good as your last picture. He should be fascinating to talk to about the business."

"Anyway," Lorna continued, "word is that Gwendoline owns a health club in Beverley Hills: aerobics, yoga, aromatherapy, that kind of thing. Naturally you've got to be super-rich to join."

"That alternative therapy stuff seems to work for her. I mean, she must be about Tyrone's age, but she doesn't look it."

"Don't be fooled, Ben. Remember, California's the home of plastic surgery, liposuction and make-overs. You can see it when you get up close to her. And she was certainly wearing a wig."

"Oh. Nought out of ten for observation. What about Rufus?"

"Ah, Rufus. The black sheep of the family. I suppose the correct word to describe him would be conman. He fled to Australia years ago to avoid some financial scandal or other. And it wasn't the first he was involved in. He's obviously back because he sniffs money."

"He likes a drink too."

"Yeah. If boozing was an Olympic event he'd win a gold medal."

"Jeremy and Belinda?"

"I think you've already got the measure of those two. He's an accountant, and I don't mean to sound cruel but he's a wimp. You saw that for yourself. Belinda dominates him totally, and she's very ambitious for him, but the material's just not there.

She's a social climber, and that takes money poor old Jeremy's expected to provide."

"That looks like one problem Felix and Crispin don't have."

She nodded. "Seems so. They're a pair of charmers, aren't they?"

"That's one way of putting it. How do they fit in?"

"They're sons of Albert Whitbourne, the eldest of Silvester's siblings. That's why they're older than us. Albert and their mother died yonks ago."

"What do they do? Apart from majoring in unpleasantness, that is."

She grinned. "Felix is a property developer. He's totally dedicated to grabbing whatever he can get. I've heard he's completely ruthless when it comes to business."

"I can believe it."

"Crispin's pretty much in the same mould. He's the only Whitbourne to live in this area, incidentally. Something to do with the local council. I think he's head of the planning department or something." She relaxed back into her chair. "And that, dear cousin, ends the rundown on our family."

"Your dad briefed you well. But I didn't know the Whitbourne's were such a bunch of grotesques. They all seem to be unpleasant, crooked or flakes."

"*All?*" she queried, giving him a look of pretended offence.

Smiling, he corrected himself. "With one or two exceptions, of course."

"That's better." She smiled back, then stared at the window. Snow fell as heavily as ever. "So what do we do now?"

The room had grown dark during their conversation and they hadn't bothered to switch on a light. If his watch hadn't had a luminous dial he wouldn't have been able to see the time. "It's nearly seven. Dinner should be any minute."

As if on cue, they heard the sound of a gong being struck somewhere downstairs.

"What a quaint old-fashioned custom," Lorna commented.

"And a movie prop, naturally."

"That doesn't surprise me! Ready to face the horde?"

"If we must," Ben sighed.

They got up and went to open the door. Neither was prepared to find a man standing outside it. Or for the burning gaze of his wild eyes. Lorna gasped and retreated a step. Ben moved forward, putting himself between her and the stranger.

"Who the hell are you?" he demanded. "And where do you get off listening at doors?"

"Wasn't listening," the man mumbled, his sombre face resentful, "just happened to be passing."

He was lean, and shabbily dressed in an old brown suit, soiled and patched. His open-necked shirt and once white trainers were equally squalid. Like his fierce eyes, his hair was jet black. Several days' stubble darkened his face.

"Well, who are you?" Ben repeated impatiently.

"Lawrence. Quentin Lawrence." The reply was grudging. "I worked for Silvester Whitbourne."

"Doing what?" Lorna wanted to know.

"Gardener, handyman. General dogsbody." His tone gave the distinct impression that the job was far too lowly for him. He regarded them with an insolent, smouldering gaze, then said, "I expect you'll be wanting your dinner. Unless there was anything else ... *sir*." He made it sound like a swear-word.

Ben shook his head.

As Lawrence turned and moved away they saw that his body was twisted, one leg dragging as he walked. They watched until he reached the end of the corridor and shuffled out of sight around a corner.

"Poor man," Lorna said.

"Yeah. I guess he's got a right to be moody."

"He's fairly young, too," she added. "Probably in his twenties, though he doesn't look it. I'd say he was quite handsome once, and pretty fit, before whatever it was that laid him low."

"I don't know if that excuses him spying on people."

"Assuming he was. I think you can be just a little bit paranoid, Ben."

"Sometimes it pays to be. Come on, let's eat."

5

The food was plain but decent, and for those who wanted it, wine was plentiful. Which kept Rufus happy.

He sat on Ben and Lorna's right. Jeremy and Belinda occupied the seats to their left. Opposite were Felix and Crispin, Gwendoline, Helena and Tyrone. Dominic Parker was seated at the head of the table. Miss Stanislavovich served, and had presumably also cooked the meal.

The spacious dining-room was decorated in typical Uncle Silvester style, with blown-up photographs from film banqueting scenes. One touch Ben particularly liked was a large picture of a young actor playing Oliver Twist, holding up his empty bowl for more.

After a stilted start, the diners began to converse more easily. When dessert was being eaten, and Olga had left the room, Lorna asked if anyone knew anything about Quentin Lawrence.

"I can tell you a little about him," Parker said, his mood more convivial than it had been earlier. "Several years ago, Silvester agreed to be one of the backers for a modestly budgeted film. This was against my advice, I might add, as investing in film making is extremely risky and often brings no return."

"You can say that again," Tyrone commented ruefully.

"In the event I was proved right and he lost his money," the lawyer continued. "Anyway, he met Lawrence when this film was being made. He was a stunt performer, and apparently good enough that everyone thought he'd make a name for himself. Unfortunately he was also rash, and some act of bravado on the film set lead to a serious accident."

"Leaving him the way he is now," Lorna concluded.

"Precisely. Lame and without a career. Although Silvester was in no way responsible for the accident, and owed him nothing, he took pity on Lawrence and offered him a job."

"I'd heard he was soft-hearted," Felix put in. It wasn't intended as a compliment.

"Lawrence was embittered at losing his livelihood," Parker explained, "and came to regard Silvester's generosity as weakness. He resented having to accept what he saw as charity."

Rufus looked up from his latest drink. "I say, he isn't due anything in the will, is he?" There was an anxious note in his voice.

"And what about that Olga woman?" Crispin said. "Does she get a cut?"

Parker held up his hands. "Gentlemen, please. You know I can't reveal such details until the content of the will is formerly revealed."

"Those stunt guys are all nuts anyway," Tyrone remarked. "Crazy sons of—"

"*Ty*," Gwendoline cautioned.

"Sorry, honey. But you know it's true."

Ben saw an opportunity to talk movies. "I'm hoping to get into the business myself, Uncle Tyrone."

"As a *stuntman*? That's not the wisest of—"

"No, no," Ben grinned. "It's special effects that interests me."

"That's more like it. There's always a call for good SFX people in the industry."

"How did you get into the movies yourself?"

"Me? Well, believe it or not, I started out as a make-up artist's apprentice, back in the old Universal studios. It wasn't what I really wanted to do, but getting into the movies is tough, as you'll find, and you take any route you can. I was in that make-up department for a couple of years before moving on, and if I say so myself, I wasn't bad at it."

"Daddy even gives *me* tips on my personal appearance from time to time," Helena declared.

Ben wasn't sure that this was a particularly good recommendation.

"Anything for my little girl," Milhouse beamed proudly.

From the looks on several other faces around the table, Ben wasn't alone in feeling nauseous.

"I tend to agree with Mr Parker," Belinda said. "The film business seems a terribly hazardous way to earn a living. It would never suit *us*, would it, Jeremy?"

"Well, I—"

"Exactly. Some people might view accountancy as drab and unexciting, but at least it's a *real* profession." Belinda noticed Milhouse's expression and hastily added, "No offence, of course, Tyrone." She looked over to Gwendoline. "You know what I mean, don't you my dear, about it being so chancy?"

"I've never given it much thought."

It was a frosty reply. Belinda coloured slightly with embarrassment.

Gwendoline pushed her plate away and turned to her husband. "I really ought to go and do my meditation, Ty."

"OK, sweetie. She always finds an hour or two for her meditation and yoga every day," he told everyone. "I wish I had as much self-discipline!" He dabbed his mouth with a napkin and began to rise.

As the others followed his example amid a hubbub of conversation, Parker tapped the side of his coffee cup with a spoon to gain their attention. "Ladies and gentlemen," he announced, his dry manner returned, "I would appreciate it if we could all gather in the sitting-room in one hour to hear Silvester Whitbourne's will. Thank you."

"And about time too," Felix whispered loudly enough for the rest to hear.

Olga appeared and started clearing the table, her face as humourless as ever.

The Whitbournes drifted to the door in groups of twos and threes, several commenting on the deteriorating state of the weather. Lorna and Ben lingered in the hall outside, watching them disperse to various parts of the house. Then they took the stairs.

"Belinda seems to have put her foot in it as far as Gwendoline's concerned," she said.

"Yeah. And Felix is hardly a diplomat either, is he?"

"No, he's not." They reached their landing. "Look, I haven't had a chance to unpack yet, and I could use a bath, so I'll see you down here in an hour."

"OK, just before nine then."

She nodded and they went their separate ways.

Ben was the first to come down.

There was no one in the sitting-room. A wide-screen television with a video recorder had been placed at one end. Several rows of chairs faced it.

His watch told him there was still ten minutes to go. He plucked a book about movie stars from a shelf and settled in an armchair by the fire. Flipping through, he stopped at a chapter on Arnold Schwarzenegger and began reading.

He was halfway through when all the lights went out.

It must have been the entire house, because he heard distant voices raised in protest. At least he had some light from the fire; other people were probably in complete darkness. But he saw no point in blundering around and decided to sit tight until things were sorted.

A few minutes passed before someone came noiselessly into the room holding a candlestick. It was Olga. He stood, and she stiffened on seeing his outline in front of the flames.

"It's me, Miss Stanislavovich," he reassured her. "Ben Whitbourne. What's happened?"

"A power cut," she replied curtly. "It would be best for you to stay here while it's repaired." Her accent turned *while* into *vile*.

"*Can* you repair a power cut?"

"Obviously you do not know that Xanadu has no mains electricity supply. It is too far from the pylons. We have our own generator, and a stand-by, but they must both have broken down."

The beam of a flashlight pierced the gloom. They were joined by a doleful-looking Quentin Lawrence.

"Ah, Lawrence," Olga said. "You will please fix the generator."

"What did you *think* I was about to do?" he replied tetchily.

"Then do not stand here wasting time," she sternly advised him.

He left without further word.

"Where *is* the generator?" Ben asked.

"In an outbuilding behind the house." Olga swept towards the door, skirt rustling, candle held high. "Excuse me while I attend to things," she said.

Alone again, Ben resumed his seat by the fire. *What the heck*, he thought. I *can't do anything so I might as well relax*.

He leaned back with his interlocked hands behind his head, feet resting on the fender in the hearth. A glance at the window showed the weather was as bad, if not worse, than earlier.

Ben stared at the unending snow. After a few minutes he found it had a kind of mesmerizing effect.

It had been a long day, what with the journey from London and everything. Now the hypnotic snowfall, the warmth from the fire and the still, quiet darkness were making him sleepy. He yawned. His eyelids began to droop.

A loud bang shattered the silence.

Shocked, he leapt from the chair. He thought it sounded like a gunshot. Then he dismissed the idea. Why would anybody be firing a gun in the house?

There were shouts. Doors slammed. People were pounding down the stairs.

Ben went out to the hall. Crispin and Felix, the latter with a pocket torch, ran towards him from the stairway.

"Was that a shot?" Felix said.

"That's what crossed my mind," Ben replied.

Rufus arrived, leading Jeremy and Belinda, who carried candles.

"I'm sure that was a firearm," Rufus exclaimed.

"What's going on?" Belinda demanded.

Parker came around a corner. He was holding a small candelabra. Tyrone and Helena thundered down the stairs, hand in hand. Almost immediately, they were followed by Lorna, who ran to Ben.

There was a confused babble as they all tried to talk at once.

"Just a minute, everyone!" Parker shouted. "Please!"

They quietened. At that moment Olga turned up. "I heard a sound. Like a—"

"Like a gun being fired?" Rufus said. "Yes, we did too." He addressed the others. "I take it everyone's agreed it sounded like gunfire?"

They were.

"Are we all here?" Parker wanted to know.

"Lawrence is outside trying to fix the generator," Ben told him.

"Where's Mom, Pop?" Helena asked.

"She said she was going to the library," Tyrone said.

Parker looked startled. "But I think that's where the shot came from."

"Me, too," Crispin added.

Several of the others nodded.

"*Come on!*" Ben yelled.

He lead the others in a rush across the hall to the library's double doors.

"Have a care!" Rufus warned him. "We don't know what might be in there!"

Ben put his ear to the wood. "Can't hear anything." He reached for the handle and tried turning. "It's locked. Is there a spare key?"

Olga came to stand beside him. "No. The only one is in the door, but we never use it anyway. Besides ... see?" She pointed. "There's no keyhole. It can only be locked from the inside."

Belinda shuddered and moved nearer Jeremy. "I don't like the look of this..."

"Everybody stand back!" Felix ordered. "Let's do it, Crispin!"

The brothers rammed the door with their shoulders. It held. Tyrone joined them. After two more assaults there was a splitting noise and the door gave.

Felix, Crispin and Tyrone tumbled into the darkened room. Ben held up his hand to stop Lorna and the others following. "Wait here," he advised. He indicated Olga's candlestick. "May I?" She handed it to him.

He went into the library.

The three men were huddled together over something on the floor. Felix and Crispin directed torches at it.

Tyrone was mumbling, "Oh my God, oh my

God…" over and over again. Felix was clutching his arm to support him.

"What is it?" Ben realized he was whispering.

Crispin turned to him. His face looked horribly ashen. "Come and see for yourself. But be warned, it isn't a very pretty sight."

Ben moved forward and they parted to let him through. Then he looked down.

It took a second for him to realize he was looking at Gwendoline. She was sprawled with her arms and legs at crazy angles in a dark wet pool. A shotgun lay beside her. Her face was almost unrecognizable. Ben looked away in disgust.

He had never seen a dead person before. But he didn't think they came much deader than the broken woman at his feet.

6

The lights flickered and came back on.

They showed the full extent of Gwendoline's wound. Tyrone gasped and hid his face in his hands. His shoulders heaved as deep sobs racked his body.

Felix caught his brother's eye. Crispin understood. "I think it'd be best if we got you away from here," he said, clutching the distraught film producer's arm.

"Perhaps we should keep the others out for now," Ben suggested softly.

Crispin turned his head and nodded as he led Tyrone from the room. The door was still on its hinges and he pulled it to behind them. A murmur of voices could be heard in the hall.

Felix expelled an audible breath and said, "There's something we ought to do." He knelt and took Gwendoline's wrist, holding his finger over her pulse. Two or three seconds passed in silence before he slowly shook his head. "Had to try. You never know."

Ben tore his gaze from the red mess of Gwendoline's face. He looked around the library. Its numerous shelves, running from floor to ceiling on every side, were packed with countless thousands of books about cinema. But it wasn't the incredible number of volumes that caught his attention.

He noticed two very odd things.

Now he could see the inside of the library door, he realized there was no key in the lock. He checked the floor, thinking the key might have been knocked out when they forced entry. It wasn't there.

At the opposite end of the room was a pair of French windows. They were wide open. The curtains billowed and a bitter wind blew snowflakes in from the garden. He walked over, aware of Felix watching him.

A smooth, unbroken layer of whiteness blanketed the ground outside. Had anyone entered or left the room there would have been footprints.

But if nobody's come or gone this way, why open the window in such bad weather? Ben wondered.

The snow was still falling heavily. But he doubted enough had come down in the last few minutes to cover any tracks so completely.

He was puzzled. His thoughts were interrupted by Felix saying, "We should close it."

"Oh. Yeah." Ben reached out. Then he stopped himself and dug into his pocket for a paper tissue.

With this around his hand he shut the window, touching the handle as lightly as possible with his fingertips.

"Why did you do that?" Felix asked, as Ben clicked home the latch.

"Because the police might not be very pleased if we disturbed the place too much."

"You mean fingerprints, that kind of thing? Surely that doesn't apply to a suicide?"

Ben realized Felix hadn't noticed the key was missing, or that there could be some significance in the French windows being open. He'd apparently jumped to the conclusion that Gwendoline had killed herself.

Perhaps she had. But it didn't look right.

Rather than comment on his assumption, Ben replied, "We'd better not disturb things, just to be on the safe side."

"I suppose that means we shouldn't touch the weapon either," Felix said, nodding at the shotgun. "I wonder where she got it," he added.

"It might be from the collection. They use real guns in films sometimes, you know. Then again, it could be one Uncle Silvester kept for clay-pigeon shooting. Maybe she even brought it with her."

"Seems an unlikely thing to pack. Unless she came with the *intention* of committing suicide. And she didn't seem particularly depressed or anything at dinner." He shrugged. "But who can say what's in some people's minds?"

"Right," Ben agreed. "Anyway, there's nothing we can do here. Let's leave it for the police, shall we?"

"Fine by me."

They came out of the room in time to see Belinda and Jeremy guiding Tyrone and Helena up to their rooms. Once they'd gone, the remainder of the group anxiously gathered around them and began firing questions.

"What's going on in there?"

"Has there been an accident?"

"Is it true Gwen's dead?"

Parker raised his hands for silence. Then he turned to Ben and Felix. "Can either of you please tell us what's happened?" he demanded. "Mr Milhouse was in a terrible state."

"Looks like Gwendoline's shot herself," Felix told them.

Rufus turned pale and slumped into a chair.

"Suicide?" Parker whispered.

"But *why*?" Lorna said. "She seemed fine earlier."

"That's for the police to find out," Ben said.

"Yes, of course," Parker agreed, "we must ring them immediately." There was a phone on a table beside the seat Rufus occupied. The lawyer plucked it up. "Damn," he muttered, rattling the receiver. "It seems to be dead."

"I'll try the one in the sitting-room," Crispin suggested. He ran off across the hall.

"The telephone lines run overground on poles in this area," Olga explained. "They often go down in bad weather."

Crispin returned shaking his head. "No joy."

"So no fax or Internet either," Ben said.

"And it's going to be near impossible to send somebody for help in these conditions," Lorna remarked. "Wait a minute! Didn't you mention having a mobile, Felix?"

"Yah, course! In the car. Crispin, go and get it."

His brother grumbled under his breath but went for his overcoat. As he was shrugging it on, Olga said, "Lawrence is out there somewhere. He has a key, but I'll listen out for you in case you don't see him."

Crispin opened the door. A blast of freezing air swept whirling snowflakes into the hall. He battled into the raging blizzard, leaving Olga to close up behind him.

Ben glanced toward the library. "It'd probably be a good idea for nobody to go in there," he told the others. "Apart from it being ... unpleasant, we should leave it exactly as it is for the police."

Rufus was pulling himself together. "How do you think they're going to get here in this weather?"

"That's their problem," Felix said. "They've got helicopters and snowploughs, haven't they?"

"Please everybody!" Parked exclaimed excitedly. "Something else has happened."

All heads turned to him.

"I was on my way to tell you all about it when that shot rang out, and—"

"Take it easy," Lorna said. "What is it?"

"When I went into the study just now I found that the desk drawer where the will was kept had been forced open. The will was still there, but we must assume it's been read. However, the video seemed to be untouched."

"Video?"

"Yes, Miss Ferguson. Your uncle's will exists both as a written document, for legal purposes, and as a video. His intention was to tell you his wishes himself, so to speak."

"Looks like there's going to be a delay before we get to see the show," Felix commented.

"Sadly, yes," Parker replied. "It would hardly be fitting to proceed this evening in view of what has occurred. But what's disturbing is the thought that someone could have got into the house and—"

"In this weather?" Rufus interrupted. "A burglar who's also an expert skier? It seems a bit unlikely, Mr Parker."

"Yes, I suppose it does." The implication hit him. "But that means it must have been someone already present! Surely not. I cannot believe that anyone here would do such a thing."

"And why would they want to?" Ben observed. "What's the point of breaking into the desk to read the will when it was about to be revealed anyway?"

The lawyer looked perplexed. "If you'll excuse me for a moment, I think I'll go and put the will and video in the safe in Silvester's office. It was something I intended anyway." He hurried off.

Rufus leaned back in the chair and closed his eyes. Felix went to sit on the bottom stair. Olga kept her vigil at the door. Each seemed lost in their thoughts.

Lorna and Ben wandered over to the other side of the broad hall together.

When they were out of earshot, she said, "You look pale."

"I'm not surprised. It wasn't too good in there."

"I can imagine. But I still can't get over why Aunt Gwendoline would want to do herself in like that."

"Funny how everybody's so ready to assume she killed herself."

Lorna was mystified. "What do you mean?"

He sighed. "I don't know, to be honest. But I *do* know that if someone decided to lock themselves in a room to commit suicide you'd expect to find the key in the door."

"You mean it wasn't?"

"No. And I couldn't see it anywhere. So unless she was so unbalanced that she swallowed it –"

He broke off. There was a commotion at the front door. Crispin was back, and Lawrence was with him. Neither seemed particularly happy.

Ben and Lorna walked over. Felix joined them. Rufus sat up.

Slipping out of his coat, Crispin announced, "The car's been broken into and the mobile phone's gone!"

"*What?*" Felix blazed. "Has anything else been taken?"

"No, I don't think so."

"Seems our burglar didn't restrict him or herself to the study desk," Rufus ventured.

"Burglar?" Crispin said.

"We'll tell you later," his brother promised. "What's more important is a phone. And I recall that at dinner Tyrone mentioned he had one in his car too."

Crispin shook his head. "I think you can forget that. Ours wasn't the only vehicle broken into. They've *all* been done. And not only smashed open either. Every one of them's been immobilized."

"Including my bike?" Lorna asked.

"*Everything*."

"Could it be local kids or something?" Rufus suggested.

Olga thought not. "Very few people of *any* age live in these parts. And even vandals wouldn't be out on a night like this."

"What the hell is going on?" Felix wondered.

"And that isn't all," his brother continued. "Lawrence here has something else to tell you."

"The generators hadn't broken down," the handyman revealed. "They'd been turned off. And I reckon the phone line going out of action was no accident either."

"Somebody's been very busy," Rufus murmured darkly.

What went through Ben's mind was: *Brilliant. As if it wasn't bad enough having a dead body in the library, now we've got no communications. And no way out.*

7

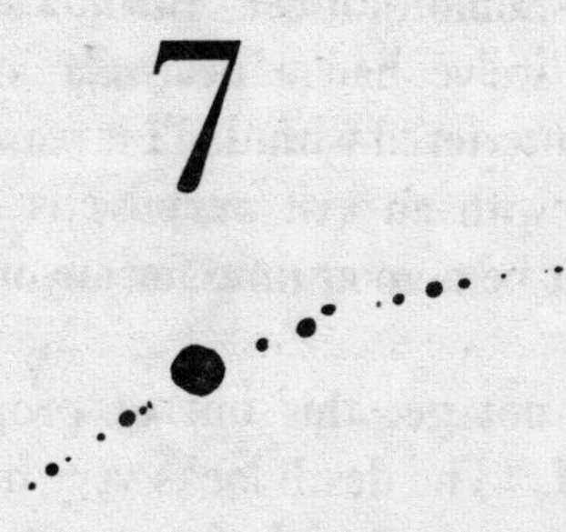

Shell-shocked, everyone except Lawrence, Tyrone and Helena gathered in the sitting-room.

Olga served coffee. Rufus and Parker chose brandy.

Putting down her cup, Belinda reported on Tyrone. "He's terribly shaken-up, of course, but fortunately we found him some sleeping pills. He was napping when I left him."

"What about the girl?" Parker asked.

"Naturally she's very upset, but not as devastated as her father. The young seem to take these things a little more in their stride, don't they?"

"Do they have any idea why Gwen should want to take her own life?" Rufus said.

"No." It was obvious from her blunt reply that Rufus hadn't risen in Belinda's estimation very much. "Jeremy or I will look in on them later," she told everyone.

Her husband nodded and sipped his coffee.

"Is it wise leaving them alone?" Felix remarked.

"Why shouldn't it be?" Belinda said.

"Well, we've had a death, a burglary and our vehicles interfered with. Isn't it reasonable to assume someone with an evil purpose is on the loose? It might not be a good time for anyone to be on their own."

"Let's not get this out of proportion," Parker suggested. "The death looks very much like suicide, even if some of us might fancy otherwise."

Ben and Lorna exchanged glances.

"And the break-in and the vandalism of the cars could just be an unrelated coincidence," the lawyer concluded.

Ben was doubtful. "It seems a very long-odds coincidence to me, Mr Parker."

"But what link could there be?"

"What if Gwendoline broke into the study desk and wrecked the cars before killing herself?" Crispin speculated.

"Why?" Lorna wanted to know.

"Perhaps there is no logical reason, any more than for her suicide. She might have had a … brainstorm, or something."

"I think Gwen was far from insane," Rufus offered, "assuming it's possible to be sure of these things." He took another swig of brandy.

A thought occurred to Ben. "Let's look at it the other way round. Suppose she *did* burgle the study as Crispin said, let's not worry about why, and found something in the will that upset her so much it pushed her over the edge. Then she ran amok and committed suicide."

Lorna shook her head. "The timing doesn't work. As I understand it, after dinner she and Tyrone went to their room and she practised her meditation while he got changed. It was only ten or fifteen minutes before the will was due to be read that she decided to visit the library. The shot was heard at about five to nine. That leaves roughly ten minutes for her to force the study desk, read the will, go outside to immobilize all the vehicles and steal the phones. Not to mention hiding them somewhere. Then she had to come back, lock herself in the library and commit suicide. It's impossible."

"You're right," Ben admitted. "And the whole thing sounds far too methodical for someone in a deranged state of mind."

"The other reason such a theory doesn't stand up is because there is nothing in the will that would have driven her to such extreme actions," Parker revealed. "Nothing immediately obvious anyway."

"We might be able to judge that for ourselves if we knew what *was* in the damn thing," Felix complained.

"It's hardly appropriate to go through it now," Parker replied frostily.

"Can't you at least give us the outline?"

"It was my late client's wish that he convey the content of his will to you all in his own words. I feel obliged to honour that wish. My suggestion is that we view the video first thing tomorrow rather than now. Out of respect to Gwendoline Milhouse and her family if nothing else."

Even Felix found it hard to argue with that.

Jeremy made one of his rare contributions. "Of course, there's the possibility that at least one person here already knows what the will says. Apart from you, Mr Parker."

For once, Belinda was caught off-balance and couldn't manage an immediate response.

Rufus took up the thread. "What are you implying, Jeremy?"

"If Gwendoline's death wasn't suicide, and it seems extremely unlikely to have been an accident, that only leaves—"

"*Murder.*" Belinda mouthed the word almost silently, in the same way some people can't bring themselves to say out loud the name of a dreadful disease.

Ben wanted to pursue this line of thought. "We have to consider the possibility," he insisted. "Because if you start looking at what happened to Aunt Gwendoline in that way, things begin to make some sort of sense. If she was murdered, then it's much more certain that the other incidents, the will, the cars, the phone line, are down to the same person who killed her."

"What would their motive be?" Felix said.

"I can only imagine it's to benefit from the will in some way. Cutting us all off from the outside world could be part of a plan. But what?"

"And whose?" Lorna added.

"Just a moment," Parker interjected. "The library door was locked from the inside. If it was murder, how do you explain that?"

"I can't," Ben confessed. "Any more than I can explain that nobody could have left via the French windows. There were no footprints outside, you see."

Murmurs of surprise greeted the news.

"But the door being locked is as strong an argument for murder as suicide," Ben continued. "Because shooting yourself is something that can be done quickly, once you've made up your mind to do it. How long does it take to squeeze a trigger? She didn't really *need* to lock the door. A murderer would, in order not to be disturbed."

"I'm far from being convinced," Felix stated. "I think it's quite possible a suicide *would* lock the door. But even if it was murder it doesn't mean it's … well, one of us. It could just as easily be an outsider. Some homicidal maniac loose in the countryside."

"Perhaps," Ben conceded.

"What I do know," Felix went on, "is that we can't sit around here doing nothing." He turned to Olga. "How far away is the nearest neighbour?"

"About a mile and a half. That is across open

country, however. The journey is hard going in the best of conditions."

"Nevertheless, Crispin and I are fit. I reckon we could make it. Don't you Crispin?"

"Frankly, Felix, no, I don't. I live in these parts, remember. You don't know the place the way I do."

"So what do you suggest?"

Parker answered. "I'm afraid our only choice is to sit tight until we can reach the outside world. This appalling weather can't go on for ever."

Then something happened that none of them expected.

The doorbell rang

"What the *hell*?" Rufus exclaimed.

"Could Tyrone or Helena have gone outside?" Lorna whispered. "Or Lawrence?"

"No," Olga said. "For the Milhouses to come from upstairs, or Lawrence from the kitchen, they would have to pass this room to get outside." She indicated the open entrance with a wave of her hand. "We would have seen them. There are two other doors to the grounds but they are both securely barred."

The bell rang again, long and persistent.

"Perhaps it's someone come to help us," Rufus ventured.

"Nice thought," Crispin said, "but how would they know we *needed* help?"

"It might be the maniac," Belinda suggested nervously.

"What, ringing on the doorbell?" Felix scoffed.

"Look, this is ridiculous. We can't just ignore it. And there's quite a few of us here; surely we can handle answering a wretched front door."

"Yes," Rufus agreed, "we should go."

They quickly decided Parker would stay with Belinda and Lorna in the sitting-room. Olga was sent to warn Lawrence, then check on Tyrone and Helena.

That left Ben, Rufus, Felix and Crispin to see who was at the door.

"Four of us should be more than enough," Felix declared. He picked up a hefty poker from the hearth. "But I'll bring this along as added insurance."

"Take care!" Lorna called as they headed for the hall.

The bell sounded yet again.

At the door, Rufus whispered, "You answer it, Ben. We'll stay out of sight until needed. Element of surprise and all that."

Ben nodded. The others flattened themselves against the walls where they couldn't be seen. Steadying himself with a deep breath, Ben reached for the bolt. He slid it aside and turned the handle, pulling the heavy, creaking door inwards.

There were two men outside, wrapped so thoroughly against the weather that he couldn't see their faces properly. One of them said something, but the words were too muffled to make out. They pushed into the hallway. A flurry of snow whipped around them. Ben hurriedly backed off.

Then there was an explosion of activity.

Felix and Rufus leapt out of their hiding places and grabbed hold of the first man. Crispin tackled the second. Ben joined in to help him. There was a confusion of jabbing elbows, kicking legs and raised voices.

Ben and Crispin's man wore a long scarf. As they struggled, it was torn away from his neck, revealing a priest's white dog-collar. They gaped in bafflement.

At that point the other man yelled, "What's the matter with you people? I said *I'm a police officer*!"

Parker read the police warrant card aloud. "Detective Inspector Terence Baldwin, CID, Cornish Constabulary."

The card's photograph showed the man seated in front of him. He was in his forties. His face was what some people might call lived-in; weather-beaten, lined and showing his age. It was topped by an unruly mop of ginger hair and framed with bushy sideburns. He wore a cheap, rumpled blue suit and scuffed suede shoes.

Handing the card back, Parker said, "My apologies again for the rough way we handled you and your companion. But I hope that under the circumstances you understand our jumpiness."

It seems a bit of a coincidence, Ben pondered, *that a policeman should turn up just when we wanted one*.

Baldwin pocketed the ID. He held out his hands to the newly-banked sitting-room fire. Faint wisps of steam rose from his damp clothes.

The clergyman sat next to him, also relishing the warmth.

Detective Inspector Baldwin looked up and realized they were all waiting for an introduction. "Oh. This is the Reverend Franklin Kimball."

"Good evening everyone," the vicar said.

The others returned his greeting. And Ben added, "Sorry about the misunderstanding, Reverend. We don't normally attack visitors."

Kimball smiled. "That's perfectly all right. No harm done." But his shrewd eyes, framed by gold wire-rimmed spectacles, avoided Ben's gaze.

Possibly in his late fifties, Kimball had flyaway, thinning white hair. He was short, and his black priest's garb went some way to disguising his plumpness.

Olga arrived with a tray and handed them coffee. Ben noticed the Inspector's bemused expression on finding his mug was decorated with a picture of Mickey Mouse.

Rufus wandered over with the brandy decanter. "How about a little something to warm you up?" he offered.

"Not while I'm on duty, thank you, sir," Baldwin replied stiffly.

Reverend Kimball held out his mug. "I think I could manage a small amount." He caught the

Inspector giving him what appeared to be a disapproving look. "Just for medicinal purposes, of course."

While Rufus poured, Belinda addressed Baldwin. "What we can't understand is how you knew we were in need of the police, Detective Inspector."

"I didn't, madam." He cradled the mug. "I'm afraid this isn't a rescue mission. The fact is that Reverend Kimball and I were nearby on … other business. My car got hopelessly bogged down in this foul weather and we had to abandon it."

"Other business?" Felix queried.

"Official police business." His cagey reply invited no further questioning. He and Kimball exchanged a glance Ben couldn't fathom.

"So we set out for the only house in the district I thought we could reach," Baldwin continued. "We nearly didn't make it. Conditions out there are the worst I've seen in years." He drained his mug and placed it on a coffee table. "And now you tell me there's been some kind of mysterious death on these premises, and other incidents. Perhaps someone could explain in more detail."

Parker did so as the policeman scribbled in a notebook.

"I'll speak to Mr Milhouse and his daughter later," Baldwin promised when the lawyer had finished.

"You're probably wondering why we're all gathered here, Inspector," Parker added. "It's for the reading of—"

"Mr Silvester Whitbourne's will. Yes, sir, I know."

"Really?"

"It's hard to keep anything confidential in a small community like this, Mr Parker."

That's the same line the minicab driver came out with, Ben remembered.

"Has the will been read yet?" Baldwin added.

"No."

"Can you give any idea of Mr Whitbourne's requests?" Kimball interjected.

Parker looked affronted. "No offence, Reverend, but strictly speaking that's no concern of yours."

"Ah, but it may be." He favoured the lawyer with one of his generous smiles. "You see, as the vicar of this parish, I knew Silvester Whitbourne tolerably well. I am also acquainted with Miss Stanislavovich here, having met her on several of my visits." The toothy grin beamed her way. "Isn't that so, Miss Stanislavovich?"

Olga nodded sullenly.

"In fact," he went on, "I intended coming to this house earlier today to be present at the will's reading. Only I, er, ran into the Inspector here and..."

"There was no mention of your attendance in the instructions my client left," Parker said.

"An oversight, perhaps. I had been led to believe that Mr Whitbourne may have earmarked a sum in his will to help with my church restoration fund."

"Mr Whitbourne's financial intentions will be

revealed in due course," Parker informed him.

Baldwin prevented Kimball from saying more by announcing, "I'll be wanting to talk to everyone, guests and domestics, at some point. But first I'd better see the body. Would someone like to show me the way?"

Before anyone else could speak, Ben volunteered. Several of the others made to follow, but Baldwin said, "I think we'll just keep it to this young man and myself. It's always best to have as few people as possible at the scene of an incident."

Ben exchanged a quick glance with Lorna and led the Inspector out of the room.

When they reached the library door, the policeman stopped, "Now, when you arrived after hearing the shot, this was locked, right?"

"Yes. It had to be broken into."

"OK." He pushed open the door.

It was pitch black inside. Ben found the light switch.

Baldwin stood looking at the body for a moment, then walked over to it. "She was just like this when you found her?"

"Yes."

"Did someone check for signs of life?"

"Felix did."

"Hm." He got out his notebook. "Nasty wound," he muttered to himself. "And the angle's consistent with it being self-inflicted. Death would have been instantaneous. Any idea who the gun belongs to?"

"No. But it could have been one of my late uncle's."

"Has anything been touched in here?"

"No. Well, except the French windows. I closed them. But I used a tissue when I did it."

"Good."

"But don't you think it's strange them being open, Inspector? Plus the fact that there were no footprints in the snow outside? And what about the missing key from that door?" He pointed back to the entrance.

"They're puzzling aspects," Baldwin admitted, "but there are probably perfectly ordinary explanations for them."

"Such as?"

"All in good time," he responded vaguely, "all in good time."

Ben was getting a little irritated with his laid-back approach. He was about to say as much when the Inspector came out with, "I've not been in this house before. I knew it was some kind of film museum because your uncle consulted the local station about security. But that's about all I knew." He regarded the well-stocked library. "Is the whole place as packed with stuff as this and the other parts I've seen?"

"Oh, yeah. In fact, the displayed items make up just a fraction of the collection. There's a vast amount stored in the basement rooms, for instance."

"I see. Funny what some people get up to, isn't it?"

Ben made no comment.

"That'll do for now. Let's rejoin the others," Inspector Baldwin suggested.

They returned to the sitting-room in silence.

Once there, Baldwin told them all, "The library mustn't be disturbed. I don't want anyone going into it before forensics can get here."

"But what's the verdict on my sister's death, Inspector?" Rufus asked.

Baldwin was scribbling in his book again. "Too soon to say."

"We don't like the thought of Gwendoline's body lying in there like that," Belinda said. "Would it be possible to move her to a decent resting-place?"

The policeman glanced up from his note-taking. "I'm sorry, no. Not until the experts have been over everything."

Reverend Kimball rose from his armchair. "But perhaps it would be appropriate for me to say a short prayer over the deceased."

"Stay there!" Baldwin snapped. Then he saw the startled looks on the others' faces and added in a more reasonable tone, "I'd appreciate it if you didn't. It's a possible scene of crime and must be left alone."

So, Ben thought, *it seems a crime might have been committed after all.*

Crispin was the next to speak. "Anyway, now that you're here, Inspector, at least we can get into contact with the outside world. I expect you'll have a team up here in no time."

"Not immediately, I'm afraid. I've no personal radio with me. There's one in my car, of course, but that's buried by snow several miles away. For now, help can't be summoned."

"Well, that's just *great*, isn't it?" Felix moaned.

"With any luck the weather might have improved by tomorrow, sir. There's not a lot we can do now. I suggest you all go to bed and I'll start a proper investigation in the morning."

"Is that the best you can do?" Felix seethed. "Tell us to go to bed and not worry that there might be a madman on the rampage?"

Parker stepped in to calm things. "You must excuse us, Inspector, but you'll appreciate it's been a trying day." Felix glared at him. "I'll have Olga prepare rooms for you and Reverend Kimball."

"Thank you, sir. I'd be grateful if you have two adjoining rooms."

Why insist on that? Ben wondered.

Belinda and Jeremy got up, and she announced, "We'll go to Tyrone and Helena. If necessary, we'll stay with them overnight."

As the other Whitbournes started to leave, Felix couldn't resist a parting shot. "And don't forget to lock your doors, everybody!"

8

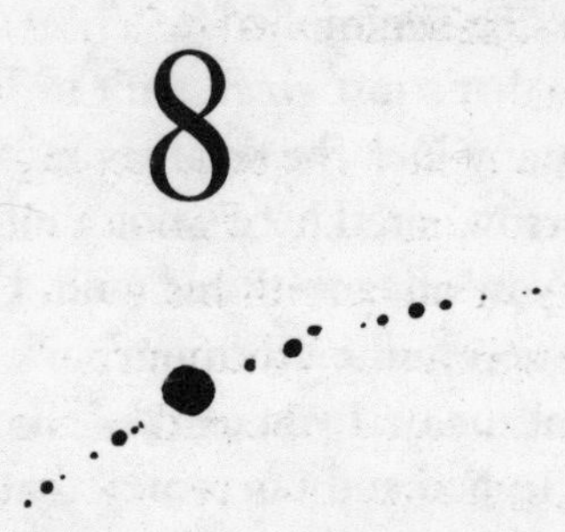

Heavy velvet curtains had been drawn to keep out the morning light. Beyond them, the snow was falling as heavily as it had the day before.

Ben sat in the second of two rows of chairs facing the giant television screen. Lorna was beside him. They were sandwiched by Olga and Lawrence, on the left, and Felix and Crispin on their right.

Seated in the front row were Tyrone and Helena, looking subdued, and in Tyrone's case, pasty-faced. The rest of the line was occupied by Belinda, Jeremy, Rufus and Reverend Kimball. Inspector Baldwin lounged at the back of the darkened sitting-room, out of Ben's sight.

Dominic Parker stood by the TV, a remote control in his hand. He cleared his throat theatrically, and having gained everyone's attention, began to speak.

"I won't waste time with a long introduction," he said.

"Good," Crispin muttered.

"Except to express what I'm sure are all our feelings in offering sincere condolences to Mr Milhouse and Helena in their tragic loss," the lawyer continued.

"Helena *Belle*," the teenager piped up.

"Er, yes. Quite so," Parker acknowledged. "And now, in accordance with his wishes, I'll hand over, as it were, to Silvester Whitbourne."

He took a seat at the end of the first row, next to Kimball, and aimed his remote at the screen. White static filled it. Then the video kicked in.

If they expected something solemn, they were mistaken.

Boom-boom, boom-boom, booom booom, *boom-boom!*

A loud, typically brassy Hollywood fanfare thundered from the speakers. The picture was of an imposing stone structure, picked out by swaying spotlights. Everybody in the room must have seen it a thousand times before. It was suddenly replaced by the head of a roaring lion in a lifebelt-shaped hoop bearing Latin words.

Most of the gathered Whitbournes were baffled. Several protested.

"*What?*"

"Surely it's a movie?"

"Is this the right tape?"

The screen now showed the Statue of Liberty, dazzling beams radiating from her raised torch.

"I can assure you there's no mistake," Parker soothed, "as you'll see in just a second."

Ben smiled as a series of images and music, familiar from the beginnings of countless films, succeeded each other. Only Silvester would have thought of starting his video will with the trademarks of all the major studios. Lorna's grin indicated that she appreciated the joke too.

The logos finished, to be replaced by Silvester, sitting at his desk in the study along the hall. A window behind him displayed a summer scene of green-leafed trees and sunshine.

He looked into the camera and greeted the living with a cheery smile.

"I have no way of knowing how many of my family are present to view this last will and testament," he began. "Many of you felt unable to visit me when I was alive. Hopefully I've drawn a better audience now that I'm dead."

"That's in rather poor taste," Belinda hissed.

Silvester went on, "So I'll assume that I'm addressing my brothers Rufus, Jeremy and Dean, my sister Gwendoline..." Tyrone shifted uneasily in his seat "...my sisters-in-law Belinda and Penny, brother-in-law Tyrone, my nephews Ben, Felix and Crispin, and nieces Lorna and Helena."

Of course, Ben thought, *he had no way of knowing my parents wouldn't be here. Or Gwendoline.*

On the video, Silvester paused. "Have I missed anyone? No, I don't think so. And as far as non-family are concerned, I'm sure Miss Olga Stanislavovich and Quentin Lawrence are there with you. That's got the credits over with. Some cast, eh?"

Ben didn't think he was going to enjoy this, but he was wrong.

"I'll start by saying that all of you stand to benefit from my will," his uncle continued. "Whether you'll benefit in the way you expected or hoped is another matter. First, we'll get the vulgar subject of money out of the way as it's a topic I know interests some of you a great deal. I leave each of the family members I've named the sum of ten thousand pounds. In recognition of their service to me, I leave Miss Stanislavovich and Mr Lawrence half that amount between them."

There was an undertone of murmured reactions. At least some of them sounded disappointed.

"In addition to this there are a few small bequests for one or two people and a handful of donations to charity. Mr Parker can provide details should any of you be interested. So much for the trailer. Now let's get to the main feature. And we'll cut to the chase, shall we?" Silvester allowed himself a brief smirk at his witticism. "As you all know, the bulk of my not inconsiderable fortune is sunk in the collection of movie memorabilia that surrounds you, and in Xanadu, where I chose to house it. The collection is my life's work, and I believe it to be unique in its scope and quantity. My wish is that it should remain intact as a monument to the art of cinema."

Attaboy! Ben thought.

"I am aware that some of you are sympathetic to my obsession, some indifferent, and others downright hostile. My problem was how to be sure who among you would act in the best interests of achieving my dream. Originally, I thought of donating the collection to an existing museum. I decided against that for two reasons. First, because I know of no such institution that would be able to display it adequately. Second, and perhaps more importantly, I want the collection to remain in Whitbourne hands, and for the family to take personal responsibility for it. In this way I hope at least some of you will grow to appreciate and value the fruits of my many years of labour."

Silvester paused again, more dramatically this time.

He always was a bit of a ham, Ben reflected affectionately.

"Therefore my decision," his uncle announced, "is to leave the collection to you all, along with Miss Stanislavovich and Mr Lawrence, who have been loyal servants, in twelve equal portions. I say twelve because I have determined that Dean, Penny and their son Ben's share will count as one. This is purely for practical purposes. To be blunt, and without wishing to cause offence, the fact that Penny and Dean are no longer together, and each so often abroad, will make it difficult for them to fulfil certain conditions attached to my inheritance. If you're present, Penny and Dean, I hope you'll understand,

and be content to let Ben represent you in this matter."

Ben was a little embarrassed that his parents should be singled out this way. And intrigued at what was to follow.

"My conditions are these," his uncle continued. "No heir can sell their share, except to another heir. The collection as a whole cannot be sold to an outsider unless all twelve of you agree to do so. Also, I would like Xanadu to be opened to the public as soon as possible. Any profits over and above the running costs can be shared between you, thus providing everyone with a source of revenue. A fund of money has been set aside to cover the collection's maintenance, and to pay for adding to it. In this respect I suggest my nephew, Ben Whitbourne, should act as an adviser on which additional items are to be acquired." He grinned. "I'm counting on you still sharing my interest in this stuff, Ben."

Ben was delighted at the honour. Lorna reached over and gave his hand a squeeze.

"Finally, some thought must be given to what happens if any of you should die. In the event of a death, the deceased's share will be divided equally among the other eleven inheritors. The same applies to any further deaths. As each of you passes on, as you reach that final reel as we all must, your portion will pass to the survivors. This in no way affects my stipulation that every one of the portion holders must agree on any decision to sell the collection." He shrugged. "Of course, you may all get together and decide to sell immediately. I can't predict that. But my hope is that those of you who see the worth of keeping the collection complete will restrain those who do not. I believe this is the best way to protect its future. I have made you the guardians of a marvellous heritage. Take the time to explore and enjoy it."

He leaned back in his chair. "I can no do more than rely upon you, my twelve beneficiaries, to respect my wishes. All that remains now, to use a term from the movies, is for me to ... *fade to black*."

Silvester Whitbourne vanished.

Instantly, a wacky fast-paced tune blared from the TV. A beaming cartoon pig appeared, hand raised in jaunty farewell, one eye winking.

"*Tha-tha-tha ... that's all, folks!*" it stammered.

And the screen returned to bright static.

The following silence was broken by Belinda's indignant, "Well, *really*!"

After the viewing of the will, Inspector Baldwin told everyone to be prepared for an interview with him. And as he wanted to see them all individually, they should expect it to take most of the day. Ben and Lorna were among the first to be seen, each spending about half an hour with the Inspector in the sitting-room. Most of the questions went over old ground.

After that, there being little else to do, Ben took the opportunity to show Lorna one of his favourite places in Xanadu.

"I loved this room when I was a kid," he said, pushing open the door.

He was pleased at her reaction when she saw what was inside.

"Wow, Ben, it's brilliant!" She rushed ahead of him and began examining the interior.

The robot room was as much fun as he recalled. Two completely shelved walls displayed hundreds of toy robots of all shapes and sizes; collectible scale models from numerous movies. There were framed posters of films featuring robotic characters. Mounted photos of Gort, the mechanical man from *The Day the Earth Stood Still*, and Robby the Robot from *Forbidden Planet* hung alongside Daleks, R2D2, Robocop and many others.

At the far end of the room a large window was guarded on either side by life-sized robots. To the left stood shiny gold C3PO. The figure on the right was a graceful female robot in equally striking silver.

"She's beautiful," Lorna enthused.

"Famous too," Ben replied. "Recognize her?"

"Course. She's one of the few female robots in the movies, a robotrix. From *Metropolis*, the German silent film."

"Right. That was made in the twenties, so she's quite possibly the first robot ever featured in a picture."

Lorna lightly touched the robotrix's elegant cheek. "It's a reproduction, right?"

"No, that's the original."

"You're *kidding*! It must be one of the rarest props in movie history."

"And almost priceless. That should give you some idea of the value of the collection."

She noticed his expression grow serious. "What's the matter?"

"I think our uncle made a serious mistake." He pointed to a small sofa in front of the window. "Let's settle and I'll explain."

The outlook was of unending snow. What they could see of the garden, a floor below, was covered several feet deep.

"What mistake?" she asked. "I think Uncle Silvester did the most sensible thing he could to preserve the collection. He even foresaw the problems of making your parents trustees, given that they've separated and spend so much time abroad. Or is that what's upsetting you?"

"No, it's not that. I get on really well with both of them, separately. But they just don't get on with each other. They'd never be able to agree on anything about the collection. What with that and their travelling ... well, it was perfectly sensible to make me their agent, and I know they'll agree. And of course I'd see to it that they benefit from any income the collection might bring in."

"Sure you would. And he even wanted you to help keep it going. You must be pleased by that."

"I *am*. But you obviously haven't spotted the flaw

in his plan. Don't you see? It only takes one of the twelve inheritors to be more interested in money than the collection. If each time someone dies their share passes to the rest, then anyone determined to turn the collection into cash has a bigger slice and less people to persuade to sell it. For somebody greedy and ruthless enough, it's an incentive to kill the others. Or at least to do away with those of us who won't agree to the collection being sold. That certainly includes me. And I'd guess you too."

"You're right; I'd never go along with it being sold. But surely no one sane could possibly think they'd get away with murdering all of us to gain sole ownership of the collection? They'd be suspect number one."

"They could if the deaths appeared to be accidents. Or suicide."

"*Like Gwendoline!*"

"Exactly. Remember, someone got to know what was in the will before the rest of us. They might also have known that Gwendoline would have been against selling the collection."

"And decided to get her out of the way at the first opportunity."

"It's possible," Ben agreed grimly. "It'd be interesting to find out exactly what Aunt Gwen's opinion on selling would have been. In fact, I'd like to know what *all* the others think."

"Hard to tell, isn't it? But I'd guess most of them would have much preferred a nice big wodge of money rather than being made guardians of the collection." She frowned. "We might be the only ones opposed to selling, Ben."

"I know. So unless I'm way out of line with my theory, that could mean we're in danger. We have to be very careful from now on, right?"

Lorna nodded. "Anyway, at least luck's provided us with a policeman. Baldwin must have realized the will's implications, the way you did, and having him around is bound to discourage your supposed murderer."

"I'm not so sure about that."

"Why?"

"For a start, he gives me the impression of being too willing to accept Gwendoline's death as suicide. Any evidence pointing to murder doesn't seem to interest him a lot."

"You said, 'for a start'. What else about him bothers you?"

"Well, assume I'm right about Aunt Gwen having been murdered but wrong about the motive. Perhaps there's something quite different going on here. In which case, how do we know that Baldwin's really a policeman?"

"Oh, come on, Ben. He showed us his warrant card."

"He showed us *a* card, yes. But have you ever seen one before?"

"No, I haven't," she replied thoughtfully.

"Neither have I. What's to say it isn't a fake?"

"By the same token, Kimball might not even be a priest."

"Precisely. Any supplier of theatrical costumes will hire you a clergyman's outfit. There are several right here in the collection, come to think of it."

"Hang on, though. Olga confirmed having met Kimball before."

"But what do we know about *her*?"

"That's true. You think it could be some kind of conspiracy?"

"I don't know what I think. Because another thing is the tension between Baldwin and Kimball. You must have sensed it."

"Yeah, I did, now that you mention it," Lorna recalled. "Yet Baldwin was keen for them to have adjoining rooms. What was *that* all about?"

"Who knows? Maybe to make it easier for them to get together and hatch plots. We shouldn't rule out any possibility. And I think it would be a good idea to watch our backs from now on."

9

Ben suggested they kill time until lunch by exploring some more of the house. Lorna readily agreed.

He decided to show her the extensive basement area. As they walked one of its corridors, she said, "I'd no idea it was so *big* down here."

"Uncle Silvester had the whole below-ground part of Xanadu vastly expanded. Most of the collection's actually on this level, boxed and filed. What's displayed upstairs is just a selection of items."

They came to a large doorless chamber lined with scores of grey filing cabinets, each bearing letters of the alphabet. Ben randomly chose a cabinet, labelled *G*, and pulled out a drawer. It was packed with sheets of thin white card divided by markers. The markers had neatly typed movie titles pasted to them; *Godzilla, Gone With the Wind, Grease…*

"Film stills," he explained. "A couple of hundred thousand at the last count."

"This place never ceases to amaze me," Lorna said admiringly. Then she leaned against the nearest cabinet and added, "You know, the more I rack my brains about our murderer, the more I'm convinced they must be insane. Assuming Gwendoline *was* murdered, that is."

"I still think it's likely she was. But insanity's too simple an explanation. I believe there's a much more logical motive, it's just that we can't see it yet."

"Your theory about the will, yeah. But if Aunt Gwendoline did die at the hands of a killer, it might have had nothing to do with the will. I don't see why she couldn't have been the victim of a good old-fashioned wacko."

"Someone in the house, you mean?"

"Maybe. Or from outside. I'm not entirely convinced this place is as cut off as everybody says."

"I know this area a lot better than you do, and it's unlikely anyone would make it. Not impossible, sure, but unlikely. And what rational reason could there be for a stranger to battle their way through this filthy weather to kill someone they didn't know?"

"Who said crazy people were rational?"

Ben mulled that over as they wandered on. Around the next corner, Lorna was intrigued by a huge iron door. "What's that? It looks like a bank vault."

"Let me show you." He pulled on the chunky lever that engaged the locking mechanism. The door swung outward. A wave of chilly air swept from the interior.

Lorna shivered. "Why's it so *cold*?"

"The room's refrigerated. Look."

She stepped forward and peered inside. Thousands of cans of film were stacked floor to ceiling.

"Uncle Silvester accumulated probably the biggest collection of movies in private hands," Ben explained. "They have to be kept at a low temperature to preserve the celluloid. And there's some really old nitrate stock in there, which is highly inflammable." He pushed the door back into place and it clanged shut. "Now come and see this."

A few paces further along they came to a pair of swing doors. They led to Silvester Whitbourne's private cinema. It had about thirty seats, and a full-sized screen with plush red curtains on either side. Identical to a genuine cinema of the 1930s, except for being smaller, it boasted a miniature Wurlitzer organ below the stage. There was even a popcorn machine.

Lorna was delighted. She went in and tried one of the tilted seat chairs, giving a squeal as she bounced up and down in it.

Ben had stayed at the entrance. Something moved on the edge of his vision to the right. He looked that way, and where the corridor crossed another, he caught a fleeting glimpse of someone. The figure was gone in an instant.

"Hello?" he called. "*Hello?*" There was no reply.

Lorna came over. "What was that?"

"Don't know. Another Whitbourne exploring the place, I suppose. And one who didn't feel like being sociable." His face darkened. "At least, I *hope* that's what it was. Bearing in mind what's been going on in this place lately, we can't be too careful."

She moved closer to him. "It's kind of spooky down here, isn't it? I hadn't felt that before. Do you think we should try following whoever it was?"

"Don't see much point. This basement area's pretty large, and a real labyrinth. We'd be unlikely to pick up their trail. Do you want to go back upstairs?"

A determined look came to her face. "No, dammit. I'm not letting fear get the better of me. But, er, let's stay close together, eh?"

He smiled. "Of course."

"Where to now?" she asked.

"Well, if you're sure you want to go on..."

Lorna nodded.

"OK. But if there's a sign of anybody we get out of here, pronto. Come on then, there's something else I'd like to show you."

Two sharp turns in the passageway brought them to another door. Beyond lay a huge, echoing room, and Lorna couldn't see what it contained until Ben found the light switches.

The gleaming, white-tiled chamber housed an enormous pool.

"Uncle Silvester was keen on swimming?" Lorna said.

"Not particularly." Ben pointed to a mass of

floating objects moored at the far end. "He had it installed for them."

She went to investigate, and when she realized what she was seeing exclaimed, "Oh, *cool*!"

It was an assorted armada of vessels, a flotilla of models built for the movies. There were galleons, battleships, cruisers and a Viking longboat. The *Nautilus*, Captain Nemo's submarine from *20,000 Leagues Under the Sea*, lay alongside an oil tanker from a James Bond film.

Few of the models were built to the same scale. So an aircraft carrier and a pirate ship, or a Chinese junk and a speedboat, were the same size. This somehow made the sight more strangely impressive.

Lorna's attention was drawn to a long sleek model that was mostly submerged. A slender fin projected from its rubbery back.

"Is that what I think it is?"

"Yeah," Ben confirmed with a smile. "It's the shark from *Jaws*. One of the remote control jobs."

"You mean it works?"

"Quite a few of them do. From over there."

He led her to a table standing by the wall. Scattered across it were several dozen hand-held remote control devices. He picked one up and showed it to her. It had an array of buttons and lights, and twin snub aerials set in the top.

"The models have their own motors, with on-board power packs. These activate and control them."

"Neat. Let's try one."

Ben looked at his watch. "We'll have to come back some other time. Lunch is about due."

"Won't we be summoned by the famous gong?"

"We wouldn't hear it. Come on, let's go."

She looked disappointed as she tagged along behind him.

They switched off the lights and left the pool.

On their way back to the stairs, walking in silence, they came to a room their uncle used as an office. The door was slightly ajar. Ben was sure it was closed when they passed earlier. There was a light on inside. They saw someone's shadow and heard a furtive movement. Lorna stiffened. Ben froze and placed a finger to his lips. Tiptoeing to the door, he peered through the crack. He watched for a few seconds, then beckoned Lorna. She crept over and joined him.

Reverend Kimball was inside. He stood by a desk with all its drawers pulled out, intently examining a pile of papers in the glow of a table lamp. Ben pushed into the office. Lorna followed. Startled, the vicar swung around, the papers dropping from his hand. "*Oh!*" he exclaimed in a tiny voice.

"Can we help you, Reverend?" Ben kept his tone cool, his face stony.

Kimball reddened. "Er ... hello, you two." He tried a weak smile on them. They didn't respond.

"Were you looking for something?" Ben persisted.

The parson's eyes briefly flicked to the discarded papers on the desktop before meeting Ben's gaze. "Uhm ... I *was* as a matter of fact. I was hoping to find a copy of a letter your uncle Silvester sent me promising that bequest to repair the church."

His embarrassment deepened when neither replied.

"I … mislaid my own copy," Kimball continued falteringly. "Thought it might be useful to show Mr Parker, you see." He cleared his throat. "I was … surprised there was no mention of the … gift in the … will … and…" The sentence trailed off.

Ben let him stew for a few more seconds before saying, "I see."

The clergyman couldn't mistake the scepticism in Ben's voice. "Well," he stammered, "it must be almost time for dinner." He stooped for the papers. "I'll just put these back before—"

"Don't bother," Ben told him. "We'll do that."

"Right. Yes. Of course." He began moving awkwardly to the door. "I'll be on my way then."

"Just a minute," Lorna said.

Kimball froze.

"Was it you Ben saw near the cinema down here earlier?" she asked.

"Cinema?" He seemed genuinely puzzled. "No. I've only been in this room, and just for a few minutes."

Ben nodded slowly. "OK, Reverend. Catch you later."

The vicar mumbled something and fled.

"Now why did I find his story hard to swallow?" Lorna commented acidly.

10

"The question is, what was Kimball *really* after?" Ben wondered. He picked up the stack of papers and went through them. "None of this seems to be particularly important. Ancient paid bills and letters to tradesmen mostly." He slapped them back on the desk.

Lorna pointed to a safe. "Presumably that's where Parker put the will and video."

"I imagine so. But it couldn't have been the reason Kimball was here. Like the rest of us, he already knows what's in the will."

He scanned the room and noticed a grey metal box mounted on the wall. It had several glowing red and green lights, and an array of buttons and switches along the bottom.

"Of course!" he exclaimed. "I just hadn't given it a thought."

"Hadn't given what a thought?"

"That Xanadu had to have a burglar alarm system. In fact, Baldwin said something about Uncle Silvester consulting the police on security. And bearing in mind how valuable the collection is, the system here must be a fairly elaborate one." He went and examined the box. "Yeah, this is where it's controlled from. Seems to be functioning all right, though..."

"So the place is alarmed. What about it?"

"Well, assuming it's a standard system, and kept turned on, it should protect all the windows and outside doors."

She gave him a quizzical look.

"Don't you see? It makes it more likely that Gwendoline's killer was someone already in the house. An intruder would have set off the alarm."

"Not necessarily. They might not bother turning it on during the day."

"It's on now."

"Maybe that's what Kimball was in here for. To turn it on again."

"You mean he's an accomplice to the murderer, and his job was to take care of the alarm system? No, hang on, I'm being daft. He wasn't let *into* the house until after the murder."

"As far as we know..."

"Hm. Yeah. Suppose at least two people are involved. One Kimball, the other a guest. The guest turns off the alarm system to let Kimball in, murder

Aunt Gwen and get out again. Then Kimball arrives at the house openly and later sneaks down here to turn it back on." He sighed. "No. It's all a bit too complicated somehow. And making it seem the system was on all the time would only confirm any suspicion that it was an inside job. It doesn't make sense."

"You're barking up a wrong tree here, Ben. *And* you're ignoring the fact that Kimball arrived with a policeman. That would rather cramp his style, wouldn't it?"

"Assuming Baldwin's really a cop."

"If he and Kimball are phoneys, that implies another conspirator. I don't buy it."

"Neither do I."

She changed the subject. "*Could* it have been the vicar you saw near the cinema earlier?"

"I only caught a glimpse of whoever it was, and I couldn't tell if it was male or female. But I don't think it was him, Lorna."

"Why not?"

"To get from the cinema to here, without running into us, would have meant a long detour. It'd probably take *me* at least ten minutes, and I know the layout really well. I don't see how he had the time to get here before us." He frowned. "I'm going to have to think about this."

"Do it after we eat," she suggested.

Dinner was a sombre, jumpy affair, made more tense

by the appearance of Tyrone and Helena. Everyone felt too uncomfortable to mention Gwendoline's death, and the Americans sat through much of the meal in morose silence.

Afterwards, Baldwin got them all to gather in the sitting-room. Olga, Lawrence and Kimball were also called in.

Once they were settled, the Inspector announced, "I thought it might be useful to give you an update on the situation." He took the notebook from his pocket and consulted a page. "I've now finished interviewing all of you, but my investigation is still ongoing. So I may well need to speak to some of you again."

Felix let out a loud sigh. Baldwin ignored it.

"As to the possibility of communicating with the outside world," he continued, "things don't look too bright. You can see there's been no improvement in the weather." He nodded at the window and the unabated white storm outside. "We've made no headway on repairing any of the vehicles, and the phones remain dead."

"But won't there be a search party out looking for you?" Belinda asked. "After all, if a police officer fails to report for duty..."

"Normally, yes." Baldwin looked a little sheepish. "Unfortunately, as this is Saturday and I was down for weekend leave, my absence won't be noticed for a couple of days."

How convenient, Ben thought. *That's exactly the*

answer he'd give if he wasn't really a policeman.

"I thought you said this was a tight-knit community, Inspector," Felix said.

"It is, sir."

"Won't you be missed then?"

"They may be tight around here but they don't go looking for trouble. No, I'm afraid we can't expect outside help for the time being."

Felix gave another exasperated sigh. "Well, it looks as though we're to be thrown back on our own resources. *Again.*" He glared at Baldwin. "However, as we're all here, perhaps we should take this opportunity to see how we stand as far as the will's concerned."

Rufus stopped pouring his latest drink. "What do you mean?"

"I've been thinking about the clause that says the collection can't be sold unless we all agree."

"This may not be the most appropriate time..." Parker interjected, glancing at Helena and Tyrone Milhouse.

"No, that's all right, Mr Parker," Tyrone told him. "Maybe it would be useful to clear the air. What do you think, honey?"

"Whatever you say, Daddy."

He and Helena swapped saccharine smiles.

"So what exactly are you proposing, Felix?" Ben put in. "As if I couldn't guess."

"I'd like to see the collection sold, and I'm not ashamed to admit it. If the rest of you have any sense you'll agree with me. Surely a large slice of cash is better than being tied to this accumulation of junk for the rest of our lives?"

"You're suggesting we vote?" Lorna said.

"Yeah. And let's get it over with now." He turned to the others. "Does anybody object?" No one did. "All right. Let's do it on a straight show of hands, for and against selling the collection. Who's for?"

He raised his hand. Rufus, Belinda, Tyrone, Helena and Quentin Lawrence joined him. Belinda regarded her husband with slack-jawed amazement. Jeremy avoided her stare and kept his hands firmly clasped together in his lap.

Felix gave Crispin an equally dirty look. "Is that everyone?" he demanded. "Crispin?"

His brother said nothing.

"Jeremy?" Belinda queried. "What the hell do you think you're—"

"All right," the Inspector briskly intervened, "it's a democratic vote and everyone can give their opinion without being bullied." Felix and Belinda turned their bitter gazes on him, but neither argued.

"Who's against selling?" Baldwin wanted to know.

Jeremy, Crispin, Lorna and Ben put up their hands.

"She didn't vote!" Felix snapped, jabbing an accusing finger at Miss Stanislavovich.

"No, Mr Whitbourne, I did not," Olga replied coldly. "I am presently undecided as to the best course of action. It is my right to be a – how do you say? – a do-not-know voter."

"As was made clear under the terms of Silvester Whitbourne's will," Parker declared, "any decision to sell the collection must be unanimous. A split vote means there can be no sale."

There was uproar in the room. Arguments broke out.

Felix strode to his brother, grabbed the lapels of his jacket and hissed, "How could you do it, Crispin? You, of all people. My own *brother*, voting against me!"

Crispin pulled himself free. "Sorry, Felix, but I'm not convinced that selling is the best option. If we did this place up a bit I think we could derive a nice income from—"

"A nice income! You little ... *rat*! Why can't you ever..."

Ben tuned out their squabble and focused on Belinda and Jeremy. She towered over him while he sat wordless and ashen-faced under the onslaught of her tongue-lashing.

Then Crispin elbowed his way across the room and stormed out, slamming the door loudly. The incident brought a moment's quiet.

Felix broke it. "This is nuts!" he complained, still angry after the row with his brother. "I'm a busy man! I've got better things to do than hang around this dump..."

"What do you expect us to do," Belinda sneered, "pray for sunshine?"

"Go and boil your head, woman!"

"*How dare you!*" She shook her husband's sleeve. "Jeremy. *Jeremy!* Are you just going to sit there and let this upstart insult me like that?"

Jeremy gave a very good impression of someone who wished he was somewhere else. *Anywhere* else.

"Oh, so you're going to set Fido on me now, are you?" Felix mocked. "If you'd house-trained him better, Aunt Belinda, perhaps he would have voted the right way!"

"I will not be spoken to like this by a shady property developer!" she retorted. "You … you … *guttersnipe*!"

Uproar returned. People were taking sides, shouting and arguing with each other. The noise level reached hysterical pitch.

"Ladies and gentlemen, please," Parker meekly pleaded. "This is hardly becoming to the occasion." He was totally ignored.

"*Pipe down, all of you!*" bellowed Inspector Baldwin.

A little later, Lorna and Ben sat in his room, having slipped away during the scene downstairs. The door was open, but the sounds of argument had died out some time earlier. Most of the guests seemed to have retired for the night.

"Well, the vote was a bit of an eye-opener," Ben said. "I didn't think we'd have Crispin and Jeremy on our side."

"No, I didn't expect that either. Mind you, I wouldn't be surprised if Crispin voted the way he did just to get at Felix. They're always at each other's throats. The real shock was Jeremy, going against Belinda like that."

Ben smiled. "Yeah, the worm turns." He checked his watch. "It's getting late and I'd like to turn in. OK?"

"Sure." Lorna stretched and yawned. "It's been another long day and I won't need to count any sheep."

"I'll see you back to your room."

"In case there's a murderer lurking about?" She caught his serious expression and added, "That'd be nice. Thank you."

In the corridor, they ran into Jeremy. He was padding along in slippers and a dressing gown that exposed pale spindly legs. There was a rolled towel under his arm.

After exchanging greetings, Lorna asked where he was going.

"Down to the basement for a swim. It's the one thing I envy about this house. Belinda's keen on us having a pool at home, but I'm afraid our finances don't run to it at the moment."

"They would if everyone had voted to sell the collection," Ben said. "Do you mind me asking why you didn't?"

"Not at all. Although I don't know if the answer will make much sense. You see, I've always admired people who have a dream, and who go out of their way to realize it. Perhaps because I've never really achieved anything in my own life."

"Oh, come on—" Lorna began.

"No," Jeremy insisted. "I'm not being falsely modest. I really have done very little that's adventurous or out of the ordinary. But Silvester did." He waved a hand at their surroundings. "He spent years building this amazing collection. This … monument I suppose you'd call it, to something he loved. I rather admire that. And I didn't like the thought of it all being broken up and swept away so that people could make money. It doesn't seem right. So I voted against." He favoured them with a shy smile.

"We're glad you did," Ben told him. "It's good to know we've got one or two allies in the fight to preserve this place."

"You can count on my support, Ben. Well, if you'll excuse me, I'd better get to the pool." He gave them a wave and set off, adding as he left, "You know, swimming really relaxes me. It helps take me away from all my everyday cares."

"*Especially Belinda*," Lorna whispered when he was out of earshot.

11

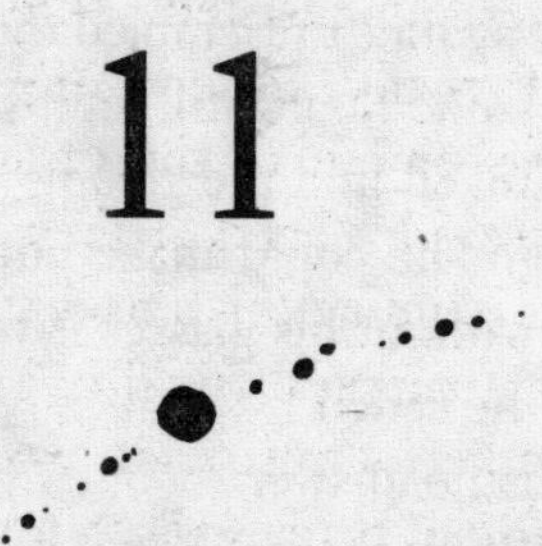

When Jeremy Whitbourne reached the swimming pool he found it dimly lit. But none of the switches would make more lights come on.

He didn't really care. In fact, he found the semi-darkness quite restful. And he liked the silence, broken only by the water's gentle lapping.

Jeremy took a quick look round the shadowy chamber, smiling faintly at the model vessels anchored at the far end of the pool. Then he dropped the towel on a bench, and removed his dressing gown and slippers. He took off his glasses and laid them down, too. With a contented sigh, he eased himself into the pleasantly warm water.

For a while he splashed around aimlessly, the sounds he made echoing wetly from the room's tiled walls. Eventually he relaxed, floating serenely on his back in the middle of the pool. The quiet was blissful, the soft mattress of tepid water more comfortable than any bed. He began to feel drowsy.

There was a faint noise from somewhere in the shadows at poolside. He thought nothing of it. The sound came again. It resembled the scuffing of a shoe against the stone floor. Still on his back, he lifted his head and blinked into the gloom.

He thought he could make out a figure near the props. But without his glasses it was only a blur.

"Hello?" he called.

There was no answer.

"*Hello?* Who's there?"

Now the indistinct figure was by the table on which the remote control devices rested. Jeremy righted himself and trod water, bobbing chest deep, as he tried to see what was going on.

He was about to call again when he heard a deep, rhythmic throb, quickly followed by a liquid churning. It came from the armada of models.

Shortly, a large, dark shape detached itself from the mass of props. Most of the object was submerged. And it was moving his way.

It began to pick up speed. Already he could feel ripples pushed ahead by its advance.

His puzzlement turned to alarm. "Excuse me!" he shouted, his voice sounding feeble and high-pitched in the great empty space. "There's someone swimming here! Don't play games! It's dangerous!"

At that moment the torpedo-shaped object passed through the weak beam coming down from one of the only working lights overhead. Jeremy snatched a view of white sleekness, and an ominous fin projecting several feet from the thing's back, cutting the water like a scythe.

He lost his nerve. Arms flailing, he executed an ungainly flip on to his chest and kicked furiously for the side of the pool. Allowing himself a quick glance over his shoulder, he saw the streamlined projectile just beyond his thrashing feet. He urged himself forward, scooping immense volumes of water aside with his aching arms.

He gazed ahead. The poolside was no more than two or three lengths of his body away. If he could just find a final spurt of energy…

Suddenly there was an enormous impact on the side of his head. Searing agony ripped through him.

Involuntarily, he opened his mouth and it instantly filled, his final shriek of pain and despair choked off.

He sank into the depths, his consciousness slipping away.

At first, Ben couldn't identify what had woken him.

He was on his bed fully-clothed, an open copy of *Great Detectives of the Movies* lying open on his chest.

The noise came again. It was some distance away, but high-pitched and persistent.

Screams?

He tossed the book aside and rolled from the bed, his sleepiness vanishing. The clock beside him, dial decorated with the picture of a gun-wielding racketeer from the forgotten gangster movie it promoted, showed that only about 45 minutes had passed while he'd slept.

Another burst of screaming rang out. And now he had no doubt that that was what he had heard. A woman, somewhere downstairs. Flinging back the door, he went out to the landing. Other people, clad in pyjamas and gowns, were pouring from their rooms. Ben saw confusion and fear on their faces.

Lorna appeared and ran to his arms. "What happened?" she asked sleepily. "Who's screaming?"

"I don't know. But it was coming from below –"

Baldwin arrived, hastily dressed in an open-necked shirt and without shoes. "Is everyone here?" he demanded.

"Olga and Lawrence are in the servants' quarters," Rufus offered. "But I don't see Jeremy and Belinda."

"We ran into Jeremy less than an hour ago," Lorna quickly explained. "He was on his way to the pool in the basement."

"Right," Baldwin said. "Let's get downstairs!"

He headed a charge down the central staircase. As they poured into the entrance hall, there were more screams, close at hand. Belinda stood at the open door leading to the basement. She was hysterical. The group rushed over to her.

"What's wrong?" Baldwin asked.

Her tear-streaked face was pure white. "Down … down there… The … pool," she whimpered, pointing to the basement stairs with a trembling hand. "It's ... Jer ... Jer ... *Jeremy*!"

"Stay with her, Mr Parker," Baldwin ordered. "I'm going down."

"What about the rest of us?" Crispin called to the Inspector's receding back.

"Suit yourselves! Just stay out of my way!"

"I'm going, too," Ben announced.

Lorna went after him. The others followed. Reverend Kimball remained with Parker, trying to help calm Belinda. Helena also stayed behind.

They thundered through the underground corridors and eventually arrived at the pool's doors. Only a handful of lights were on, and the others couldn't be made to work. In the weak illumination they could see two shadowy objects floating just beyond the pool's edge. Inspector Baldwin produced a flashlight. Felix brought out another. They directed the beams at the water.

The smaller object was Jeremy Whitbourne. His arms and legs were spread-eagled, his eyes wide open. He seemed to be staring glassily at the ceiling. The expression on his face was far from pleasant. By him drifted the prop shark.

"My God!" Rufus gasped.

Several of the guests waded in and pulled Jeremy out. Once they had him on the poolside, Baldwin set to work checking for signs of life.

After a few minutes he stood again and announced, "Dead. And from the look of him, he drowned."

"He seems to have taken a heavy battering, too," Crispin observed.

"Yes, but I imagine he got that when the shark collided with him. It wasn't the cause of death. Can somebody find something to cover the body with?"

Felix went off to unpeg a nearby shower curtain.

Miss Stanislavovich and Lawrence came through the door. When she saw Jeremy's corpse, Olga's hand flew to her mouth. "Oh no! Has there been an accident?"

"It could have been an accident, I suppose," Baldwin said. "But the odds are very much against it. Do you have a key to this room?"

Olga nodded and dug into her pocket. Felix came back with the plastic curtain and laid it over Jeremy.

Then Baldwin ushered everyone out and locked the door. "That's another one for the pathology boys," he sighed. "Whenever they can get through the cursed weather."

Those who had got wet retrieving Jeremy's body changed their clothes. Belinda was taken to her room by Olga and Rufus, who stayed with her. Baldwin got the others together in the spacious sitting-room. And quickly established that no one had an alibi for the time of the latest death.

"Belinda Whitbourne is still semi-hysterical," he explained, "but she managed to tell me that she'd grown anxious about her husband taking so long in the pool and went to look for him." He turned to Ben and Lorna. "And from what you've said, it seems you two were the last to see him alive."

"Apart from his murderer," Lorna corrected him.

"Quite so."

Ben didn't like the tone of Baldwin's voice.

"What did you talk about?" the Inspector wanted to know.

"Not much," Ben replied. "Just that he was going for a swim, really."

"Did he seem upset or agitated in any way?"

"No. Quite the opposite, in fact. Why?"

"Because I have to take into account the possibility of suicide."

"Head-butting a model shark seems a bizarre way of doing it," Ben commented drily.

"As it happens, I agree with you. I'm almost certain Jeremy Whitbourne didn't take his own life, and it's unlikely to have been an accident either."

"So surely that puts Gwendoline's death in a new light, too? You can't still believe she committed suicide after this."

The policeman stared hard at Ben. "It certainly increases the chances that we're looking at a double homicide," he confirmed. "And I have the same problem with this death as the previous one. Again, no one can *prove* where they were when it occurred. In theory, anybody under this roof could have slipped down to the pool and committed the murder."

There was a murmur of protest. Tyrone cut through it. "Anybody, Inspector? Even Belinda?"

"In a murder investigation of this kind, Mr Milhouse, no one is above suspicion."

"It wouldn't surprise me at all," Felix muttered.

Baldwin raised an eyebrow. "I beg your pardon?"

"Well, from what I've heard, Jeremy had a hard time paying the bills for her social climbing. And we all saw the way they fell out earlier tonight. Maybe she grabbed the chance to increase her share of Silvester's estate."

"Those are very serious allegations, sir."

"I'm not *alleging* anything, just making an observation. And of course there was that unfortunate business with his clients a couple of years ago. Perhaps there's a connection."

"What unfortunate business?"

"Oh, didn't you know? I believe the police were involved in some way. Seems there were questions about how Jeremy's accountancy practice handled its clients' money. There were never any criminal charges. But you know what they say; there's no smoke without fire..."

"I think that's enough speculation for now, sir. No doubt all avenues will be explored in due course. But there's not much we can do tonight. Tomorrow we'll look into the possibility of sending somebody out for help, no matter how bad the weather. With this turn of events, it's worth considering." He scanned their anxious faces. "Until then, I must insist that you all keep your rooms securely locked tonight. And don't answer the door. For *anybody*."

12

Ben and Lorna found themselves walking up to the bedroom in company with Helena. When they got to their landing, Ben asked what she thought about everything that had happened during her stay.

"Exciting, isn't it?" she lisped.

"*What?*" blurted Lorna.

"All the mystery and intrigue, I mean. As a matter of fact, this situation rather reminds me of the plot of a movie I auditioned for once."

"Did you get the part?" Ben asked. From the corner of his eye he noticed Lorna giving him an exasperated look.

"No," said Helena, frowning. "They were obviously jealous of my talents."

Lorna was determined to get back to the point. "There's nothing very glamorous about people dying, surely? I mean, good God, you've lost your own mother!"

Helena assumed a sad expression, raising her chin slightly in a pose of heroic tragedy. "Yes, that is my burden," she whispered huskily. Then, returning to her normal, insufferably cute voice added, "But, as they say in the movies, 'When you gotta go, you gotta go'. And as far as Uncle Jeremy was concerned, well, he was a bit of a wrinkly, wasn't he?"

Ben couldn't believe his ears. "Just because he was getting old doesn't mean he deserved to die, Helena."

"Helena *Belle*, if you don't mind, Ben," she sniffed. "Anyway, as far as I'm concerned, one less relative means more money for the rest of us. It's tough on Jeremy having his lights turned out like that, sure, but it's a dog eat dog world, baby."

Ben winced.

"Talking of money," Lorna ventured carefully, "do you have any idea which way your mother would have voted over selling the collection?"

"Not really. But I guess she would have agreed with me and Dad, and you know how *we* voted. I mean, who wants a stake in a dusty old museum? Give me the dough any time!"

"No offence, Helena ... er, Helena *Belle*, but I wouldn't have thought money was too big a problem when your father's a Hollywood movie producer."

She pouted. "It wouldn't be if his last four pictures hadn't bombed. And going through drama school in LA's really expensive, you know? Not to mention tap classes, my manicurist, reflexologist, personal hairdresser and make-over artist. Which reminds me, I should be catching up on my beauty sleep."

About a century's worth should do it, Ben estimated.

"Catch you later!" Helena chirruped.

"Yeah," Ben said. "Don't forget to lock your door."

She swept away, her ears no doubt ringing with imagined applause.

Lorna expelled a breath. "Beneath that winsome exterior there beats a heart of solid iron."

"Yeah. Her reaction to her mother's murder certainly seems a little on the callous side. But maybe she's just naturally selfish. I've read enough about actors to know some can be very self-centred."

"She's utterly heartless, if you ask me."

"It could simply be shock, Lorna. Different people react to tragedy in different ways, you know."

"Yeah, yeah, I know. Maybe we should give her the benefit of the doubt."

They came to his room. "Want to step in for a while and chew the fat?" he asked.

"Sure. Provided you escort me home afterwards."

Once they'd settled, he said, "So, now we know for a fact that Tyrone's had a run of box-office flops. What with that and his money pit of a daughter, it looks like he could use some cash."

"You mean, he's a suspect?"

"Isn't everybody?"

"What do you think of the idea that Belinda could have killed Jeremy? If it's true he was struggling to pay for her lifestyle, she might be tempted to do him in for his share of the inheritance. Not to mention any life insurance he may have had."

"That would make her Gwendoline's murderer too," Ben said, "and the motive for that's not so clear cut."

"It is if we stick to your original theory that the killer's one of the heirs, intent on eliminating the others. Do you think the trouble Jeremy had with his clients could have anything to do with his death?"

"How could it?"

"Suppose he embezzled money from them, lost it somehow and couldn't pay it back. Maybe Belinda thought it was time to get them off their backs."

"And killed her own husband to do it? Takes some swallowing. I'm more interested in why Felix should have brought up all that stuff about Jeremy's problems."

"Could be because he's a trouble-maker, pure and simple. Then again, it might have been to turn the spotlight on to somebody else."

"That occurred to me, Lorna."

"And the most important thing we shouldn't lose sight of is that Jeremy died just a couple of hours after voting against selling the collection. Kind of supports your theory, doesn't it?"

"Yeah. It means Crispin should look out for

himself too."

"Not just Crispin. Don't forget, we voted to keep the collection together as well. That makes us prime targets."

When it was time to see Lorna back to her room, Ben went to his door and opened it. Then he put a finger to his lips and *shushed* her. Two people were having a conversation in the corridor outside.

Gently easing back the door, Ben and Lorna peeped out. Tyrone and Quentin Lawrence were huddled together a little way along the landing. They had no idea they were being overheard.

Milhouse was saying, "...surprised that you voted with the rest of us to sell the collection, Quentin. I would have thought you'd go the other way out of loyalty to your late employer."

"I felt no loyalty to Silvester Whitbourne, Mr Milhouse, if you'll excuse me saying so."

"But why not?"

"Because he was responsible for the state I'm in. It happened on the set of the film he was financing, you know."

Tyrone nodded.

"They cut corners on that movie, Mr Milhouse. They slashed the safety limits to save money and I took a bad fall. Silvester could have prevented it and didn't. Then once I was crippled he offered me charity – a lousy job in this place. I'm owed compensation for the loss of my livelihood, the ruination of my life, and voting to sell seemed the only way of getting it."

"Well, that didn't work out. What are you going to do now?"

"That's what I wanted to talk about. Do you remember what we discussed this afternoon? Your new picture, and how I might have a part in it?"

"Now hold on there, I didn't say you could be in the movie. I just said I'd think about it. And this may not be a good time to discuss it, what with Jeremy getting offed and everything."

He made to leave. Lawrence grabbed his arm.

"Just give me a minute. I was one of the best stunt performers in the business, Mr Milhouse. And I can still cut the mustard, even with this twisted body. If you're making an action adventure pic, I'd be an asset to you."

"Let me be brutally honest with you, Quentin. Quite apart from the fact that you're … not the man you were, I have to think about the studio, the insurance people, the unions. I can't see any of them being too keen on the idea of my hiring a…"

"A cripple? It's OK, you can use the word. Everybody else does. But don't you see? The fact that I'm disabled is a great selling point. Think of the publicity. And it'll earn you Brownie points with the politically correct crowd, too. Help build your image as a socially concerned producer – the human face of Hollywood and all that."

Tyrone looked thoughtful. "Hm. There could be

some mileage in that angle."

"Just give me the chance to prove I'm as good as ever I was. That's all I ask. Let me give you a demonstration. Right here in Xanadu. Tomorrow."

"I don't know, Quentin..."

"What have you got to lose? Just make a little time for me in the morning and I'll show you what I can do."

"Well ... OK. But bear in mind this place is a booby-hatch right now and your demonstration's likely to be cancelled if anybody else gets clobbered before then."

Lawrence gave a rare smile. "Of course. Thanks, Mr Milhouse. You won't regret this."

He hobbled away. Tyrone went off in another direction to his own room.

Ben silently closed the door and turned to Lorna. "Whatever Lawrence has in mind, I'd like to be there when he tries it."

13

The night passed without incident. But it was unlikely anyone got much sleep.

Breakfast was low-key, most people eating lightly or managing only coffee. Belinda stayed in her room, bedridden with shock. Olga tended her.

When the frugal meal was over, Baldwin addressed the sombre gathering.

"My investigations earlier this morning leave me in little doubt that Jeremy Whitbourne's death is at the very least highly suspicious. On examining the pool, I found a number of the lights had been deliberately disconnected. And there's no way that model shark could have been activated by accident. It seems probable we're dealing with a double murderer."

"And what do you intend *doing* about it?" Felix demanded.

"My investigations are continuing, sir," Baldwin

replied sternly. "And just as soon as there's a lull in this atrocious weather we'll send for help." He glanced at the window. "It seems a little calmer this morning, but not enough to venture out very far."

"But who do you intend should go, Inspector?" Rufus asked. "Because if you're looking for volunteers, I shouldn't expect too much of a rush. After all, most of us don't even know the area."

"I appreciate that, sir."

"Is the phone still dead?"

Baldwin nodded.

"I've been thinking about that," Ben ventured, "and it seems logical that the killer or killers are responsible for it not working. A way of keeping us isolated, like vandalizing the cars."

"That had occurred to me," Baldwin replied. "But it's a reasonable bet the killer wouldn't have thought it necessary to interfere with other lines in the area, even if it were a practical proposition. So if this damn weather would just –"

Lawrence appeared at the door. It was the first time Ben had seen him looking excited. "I'm almost ready, Mr Milhouse," he said, shuffling towards the producer. "Another half-hour and I'll be set. OK?"

"Set for what?" Baldwin asked suspiciously.

Tyrone seemed embarrassed. "Ah yes, Inspector," he said, "I haven't had the chance to mention to you all that Quentin here is going to lay on a little demonstration of his stunt skills."

"He's going to do *what*?"

"I know it might seem slightly inappropriate under the circumstances—"

"You're telling me! We're in the middle of a siege, man, not to mention a major murder investigation."

"Look at it this way, Inspector Baldwin; we're all going stir-crazy stuck in this place and we could do with a distraction. And as the weather's slightly better, this could be the only chance we get. I might add that Quentin is putting on this demonstration in connection with a new movie I'm planning. You wouldn't want to hamper my business plans, would you?"

"This is going to take place outside?" Parker asked.

"Yes," Lawrence told him. "And it's perfectly safe, as you'll see when I'm ready." He shot a pleading expression Tyrone's way. "It won't take very long either, will it, Mr Milhouse?"

"No, that's right. Come on, Inspector, it'll take everybody's mind off the last couple of days."

"Well, I can't prevent any of you doing what you want," Baldwin sighed, "providing you don't break the law in the process. But quite honestly, Mr Milhouse, things are difficult enough here already without turning the place into a three-ring circus. If you must do it, get it over with. Be warned, however, that if I think you or Mr Lawrence are doing anything to obstruct my investigation I'll order you to stop."

"That's fair enough. Quentin, go finish your preparations."

The handyman smiled like a delighted youngster.

"I'll let you know when I'm ready," he called, as he shuffled off.

The guests went to take more coffee in the sitting-room. Several complained about Tyrone and Lawrence staging a piece of cheap entertainment in the middle of a crisis. But Ben was sure they'd all turn out to watch it.

Reverend Kimball, cup in hand, positioned himself at one of the windows. The snow had begun falling again, although lightly.

Then he said something that took everyone by surprise. "I wonder if the unpredictable weather we have in these parts will affect the theme park." The comment was directed at no one in particular.

"Theme park?" Ben said.

"Yes. Perhaps it isn't general knowledge yet, but an entertainment company wants to build a large leisure complex somewhere around here."

By now everyone's attention was on him.

"I know nothing about this," Parker confessed. "Where did the information come from?"

"Silvester Whitbourne told me. He knew because the people who want to build it had contacted him with some kind of proposition concerning the collection. An offer I believe he turned down."

"Just a minute," Ben interjected. "You're a property developer, Felix. Did you know about this?"

His cousin paused before replying, "Yes, I did. As a matter of fact, I'm hoping to have some kind of involvement."

"Why didn't you mention this before?" Rufus demanded.

"I make it a practice never to discuss future projects."

"But you should have discussed *this* one with *us*," Ben said. "Because I'd guess you were hoping that Xanadu and our uncle's collection would be part of the theme park. And I reckon that if the vote had gone your way, you would have suggested we sell to the leisure company building the park. Or maybe to a company you own yourself in which your involvement was disguised. Am I right?"

Felix reddened with anger.

Bull's-eye, Ben thought.

"All right, I admit that it had … crossed my mind to put forward the theme park company as a possible buyer. I'm a developer, it's my job to turn assets into profits. And I would have got us a good price. Everyone would have benefited."

"But we would never have known if you'd got a good price or not, would we? Because you kept all this a secret from us."

"Do you have any idea why Uncle Silvester turned down the offer, Reverend?" Lorna put in.

"I believe he thought the plan would have cheapened the collection. He considered the idea they put to him rather vulgar."

Ben glared at Felix. "So you were prepared to go ahead with a scheme for this house and its contents when you knew Silvester didn't approve. That sounds pretty shoddy to me."

"Oh, get off your high horse, Ben. There's money to be made here, once this place has been rebuilt and refurbished. I'm afraid none of you has the necessary business expertise to see that. But now this has come out into the open, I'm glad. It means I can ask those of you who voted against selling to reconsider. I can assure you that you'll get a very handsome price for your shares."

"I wouldn't want to sell my share under any circumstances," Ben announced, "and certainly not to support something Uncle Silvester was against. Even if I end up the only one who feels that way, you've lost, Felix. It has to be a *unanimous* decision."

"And Ben *isn't* the only one who feels like that," declared Lorna. "I wouldn't sell either."

Rufus knocked back the dregs of his current drink and pitched in with, "Just a second. If I remember correctly, Crispin here is head of the local council's planning department. No doubt that committee would have to approve the building of this theme park. A theme park your brother may well have a financial interest in. I trust there isn't a conflict of interests there."

"Hey, just a minute," Crispin flared. "I don't like what you're implying. And remember, I voted *against* selling. Would I have done that if I was conspiring with my brother to cheat you all?"

"I'm surprised at your attitude, Rufus," Felix

added. "After all, you voted in favour of selling. What's your problem?"

"I haven't changed my mind about selling. It's just that, when I'm playing poker, I like to know the deck isn't marked, if you know what I mean. The honourable thing would have been to tell us about this theme park before the vote."

Tyrone chimed in. "I agree. We had a right to know what you were planning, Felix."

"That's not the way I work. I like to keep control over my investments."

"You wanted it all for yourself in other words," Rufus said.

"Yes, and why not? You would have done the same."

"Perhaps. But I think the difference between us is that my greed has its limits."

"Except when it comes to booze," Felix sneered. "And where do *you* get off prattling about honour? How honourable was it for you to take off for Australia after that little financial scandal a couple of years ago? And why are you back now? Perhaps you've been selling shares in another imaginary gold mine and need money to get yourself out of a hole again!"

Ben noticed Inspector Baldwin seemed to be taking particular interest in this exchange.

And at that point the policeman decided to intervene. "That's enough, everybody! No purpose is served by this constant bickering and name-calling. If any of you have specific accusations to make about each other, or evidence of wrongdoing, I'd be obliged if you came to me about it. In the meantime—"

"Excuse me."

Everyone turned. Quentin Lawrence was back.

"Ready whenever you are," he told them.

Ben was irritated at the break-up of an argument that was yielding some interesting information. On the other hand, Lawrence's untimely interruption allowed a dangerously heated situation to cool down.

And now they were out in the garden they were all cooling down even further. To below freezing point.

Snow fell steadily. Clad in thick, warm clothing, they were gathered a short distance from the house, stamping their feet and rubbing their hands. Lawrence, dressed in a black roll-neck, black trousers, trainers and gloves, stood before them.

He pointed to a low wall. "On the other side of that is an air-bag to break my fall." Then he pointed up at the taller of Xanadu's towers, the base of which was also beyond the wall. "I'll be coming from the top window there, three storeys up. Now if you'll bear with me, ladies and gentlemen, I'll get into position."

Lawrence hurried into the house as fast as his trailing leg allowed him.

"Ben," Lorna whispered, "why are we standing in the open in sub-zero temperatures waiting for a madman to throw himself out of a window?"

He smiled at her. "It makes a change from being

cooped up in the house waiting for somebody to slaughter us."

"I do hope that *silly little man* doesn't keep us standing here too long," Helena complained from the back of the small crowd. "This weather's hell for my skin."

"Anyone for a snifter?" Rufus offered, waving a hip flask.

The window in the tower far above was thrown open. They could just make out Lawrence's white face against the dim interior.

Lorna nudged Ben and nodded towards the main house. The building came out at an angle, affording a view of the tower. Olga and Belinda were watching from a bedroom, their faces pressed against the frosty glass.

Lawrence had climbed on to the windowsill. His arms were outstretched.

Through the biting wind, they could just hear him shout, "*Here I come!*"

He paused on the ledge for a second.

Then jumped.

14

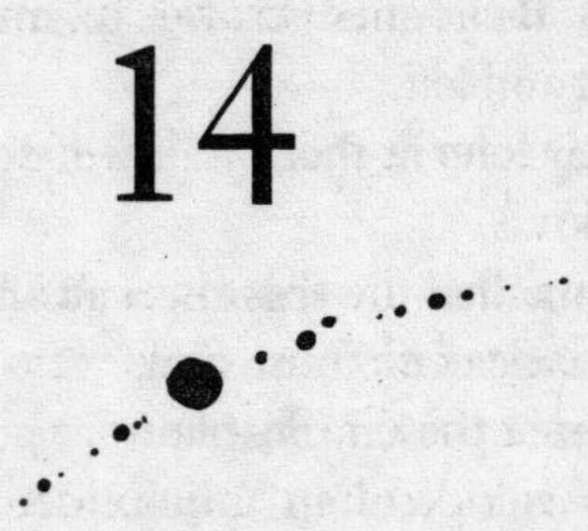

Lawrence seemed to fall for ever.

He twisted and tumbled through the air, giving an excellent impression of a man who had been pushed rather than jumped.

The crowd gasped. His plummeting body vanished behind the wall, out of sight of the spectators. There was a weighty *thrummmp*. A little flurry of snow puffed up above the brickwork.

The guests clapped, and there were ragged cheers.

"He's good," Lorna enthused. "Going to give him a job, Uncle Tyrone?"

"I might. He certainly seems to know his craft."

They waited for Lawrence to reappear.

"Where *is* he, Daddy?" Helena demanded.

"I don't know, honey. But he's a showman. I expect he's letting the tension build before making a big entrance to take his applause."

Put that way, Helena could understand. "Yeah, always milk the audience, that's what I say."

There was still no sign of Lawrence. An awkward silence came over the group.

"How long does it *take* to milk an audience?" Rufus grumbled.

"Not as long as this," Baldwin decided. "I'm going to get him."

He crunched towards the wall and around its open end, disappearing from view.

A minute passed. People were getting fidgety.

"This is ridiculous!" Felix declared. "Let's turf 'em out and get in from this wretched cold!"

If only for a reason to move and keep their circulations going, the others followed him. When they all reached the wall and turned its corner, Baldwin blocked their path. He looked grim.

"What's going on?" Parker asked. "Did he fall badly?"

"You could say that." The policeman stepped aside and let them see what was behind him.

Lawrence was spread-eagled on the ground, his arms and legs bent into crazy, grotesque angles. A vivid red stain soaked the snow.

"My God!" Rufus gasped.

Tyrone clutched wide-eyed Helena to his side. "What happened? Did he miss the air-bag?"

"No," Baldwin informed him. "It wasn't there to be missed. Somebody went to a great deal of trouble to remove it and disguise the fact with a layer of snow. Which wasn't enough to protect him from the paving-stones underneath. The impact killed him."

Lorna squeezed Ben's arm. "Oh no," she whispered, "not another one."

Baldwin scanned their anxious faces. "I want you all back inside. Now."

"What about the body?" Felix said. "We can't leave it out here."

"Good point, sir. Perhaps you and your brother would be kind enough to help me get it inside."

"I'll fetch a blanket," Crispin offered.

The others began heading after him. Parted from Lorna, Ben found himself at their rear. He brushed against a large rose bush in the flower bed facing the back of the house. Looking down, his eye was caught by something shiny entangled in its bare branches.

Baldwin and Felix were on the other side of the wall. The rest of the guests were moving away.

Carefully, he took his discovery by its edges and gently freed it. After a quick glance he slipped it into the pocket of his overcoat.

Once Lawrence's body was laid on the bed in his room, Baldwin, Felix and Crispin returned to the others.

"I was afraid no good would come of this, Mr Milhouse!" the Inspector raged. "I should never have allowed it!"

"Oh, come on," Tyrone protested, "how the hell was I to know –"

Olga entered the room and he broke off.

Baldwin turned to her. "Ah, Miss Stanislavovich. We noticed you and Mrs Whitbourne watching from the windows as Lawrence jumped. Did you see anything that might help my investigation? Anything suspicious *before* he made the jump, for instance? Anyone hanging around outside perhaps?"

"No, Inspector. All we saw was Lawrence falling and striking the ground. It was only when he didn't move that we realized something was wrong. Belinda Whitbourne did not need to witness such a horrible sight. She has much sadness already. Lawrence's death has made her feel bad again."

Not for the first time, Ben wondered exactly where she came from to have an accent like that.

"I should rejoin her," Olga continued. "It is not a good time for her to be alone."

"It isn't a good time for *anyone* to be alone," Baldwin said. "Thank you, Miss Stanislavovich. Don't linger on your way back."

She swept out of the room.

"What's puzzling me," Rufus commented, "is who could have moved the air-bag without the rest of us noticing his or her absence. Presumably it's something that would have taken a little while to do. Yet no one here seems to have been out of sight long enough."

"Could you swear to that?" Baldwin asked. "Because I couldn't. And as I understand it, Lawrence set up that air-bag at least an hour before he jumped. Enough time in theory for someone to have interfered with it."

"Obviously I've not been keeping tabs on everyone," Rufus admitted, "but it's still difficult to believe anybody could have gone out and come back again without any of us noticing."

"Perhaps not. Now we should search the house from top to bottom, to make sure no one's got in. Then we'll think about covering the grounds. It's something I should have organized before now."

"Yes, you should," Crispin agreed, an edge of sarcasm in his voice.

"Don't forget that none of us should be alone if we can help it," Ben said. "Let's search in groups of at least three, on the principle that in any pair of people one could be the murderer."

"Unless there's *more* than one murderer," Felix observed.

"Then we might just as well all blunder around in a mob. Three person groups are more manageable. And don't overlook the fact that if anything does happen to one of the groups, the killer or killers would only be drawing attention to themselves."

"And three to one is good odds for handling an intruder, should we run into one," Lorna added.

"What exactly *should* we do if we find anyone?" Rufus wanted to know.

"Raise the roof," Baldwin replied. "Make enough noise to attract the rest of us. Corner them if you can, but only tackle them head-on if you have to. Now let's sort out these groups."

They decided on Felix, Crispin and Baldwin; Ben, Lorna and Rufus, and Parker, Kimball and Milhouse. That left Helena.

"Perhaps you'd like to join Olga and Belinda?" Rufus suggested.

"No," Tyrone said. "I want my little girl with me. She can be part of our group."

"Thanks, Daddy." She beamed at her father.

Baldwin allotted a section of the house for each group to search.

Milhouse had something to say about that too. "You have your group down for searching the ground floor, Inspector, including the library. I'd prefer to do that myself, if you don't mind. My Gwen's lying in there and I think it's only right and respectful that the room should be checked by me. No offence, but I don't like the idea of just anybody barging in. It's her resting-place, after all."

"Of course. You think you'll be up to doing it?"

"I'll be OK. Let's get it over with."

They went to the library. Milhouse wanted to go in alone. Baldwin agreed as long as the door was left ajar. "And just yell if there's anything out of the ordinary. We'll be right here."

Tyrone nodded and entered. He was out again in half a minute, dabbing at tears, and whispered, "All clear." Helena took his hand.

The search parties set off.

Ben, Lorna and Rufus had been given Xanadu's

upper floors to search. The last room they went into on the top storey was packed with electronic equipment, computers and viewing screens.

"Uncle Silvester's editing suite," Ben explained. "It contains everything you'd need to cut a film or videotape. State of the art stuff, most of it. You can dub in music, design your own credits, you name it. He probably put together his video will in here."

"It's really impressive," Lorna said, admiringly.

"And of very little interest to me, I'm afraid," remarked Rufus. "I'm going to take a look out of that window in the corridor. There's a good view of the grounds and I might spot someone down there. You two take a break for a couple of minutes and explore in here."

"OK," Ben said. "But be careful."

Rufus smiled at them. "We know there's no one on this floor. And I'll be near enough to shout if I need you."

He left the door open, walked to the window and leaned on its sill with his back to them.

Lorna whispered, "Well, Lawrence's death rather dents your theory, doesn't it, Ben?"

"How come?" He was whispering too.

"He voted for selling."

"That doesn't mean anything. For someone determined to have all the inheritance for themselves, it might not matter how the others voted. They'd still have to be eliminated if the killer's eventually to control the whole collection."

"Someone who wants it all. Like Felix?"

"Maybe. Then again, perhaps there was a different motive for Lawrence's killing."

"Oh God, don't make this more complicated than it is already!" She glanced at Rufus. He hadn't moved. "But one thing's been bugging me."

"Just one?"

"All right, lots of things. But one at the moment. If the murderer succeeded in killing all of us, assuming that's their intention, how would they explain away the carnage? A house full of dead people and one survivor could be a bit of a give-away."

"Some attempt's been made to make the murders look like suicide or accidents."

"Yeah, but even Baldwin doesn't buy that any more. And who's going to believe so many people died by coincidence?"

"I don't know what's going on here, Lorna. But somewhere, in the back of my head, I'm starting to see a vague pattern. Don't ask me what it is because I don't know myself yet." He snapped his fingers. "Almost forgot. I found this." Thrusting a hand into his jacket pocket, he produced something and gave it to her.

It was a small brass key. A thin key-ring looped through a hole at the non-business end.

"Where did you come across this?"

"Out in the garden earlier. It was caught by the ring in a bush not far from the house. Look at that stuff on it."

Lorna held up the key and examined its shaft. She noticed a faint dark stain and touched it gingerly with her finger. "It's … sticky. What is it?"

"I don't know. But I've got a feeling I *should*. I've seen gunk like that before somewhere, but I can't place it."

"Are you making the same guess I am about which lock this fits?"

"Probably. I found it within throwing distance of the French windows leading to the library."

Lorna looked again to make sure Rufus was still lounging at the window. He was, but she leaned closer to Ben anyway. "I can't get my head around that locked library. Finding the key in the garden only makes sense if Gwendoline committed suicide after tossing it out there herself, and that's daft. Even if there was another key, the killer couldn't use it because the door only locks from the inside."

"Right. And they couldn't have gone out of the French windows without making footprints. Unless we're dealing with a homicidal bird." He pointed to the key. "So that mark, whatever it is, could be significant in some way."

"It's not *blood*, is it?" She looked alarmed.

"No, I'm sure it's not."

"Have you shown it to Baldwin?"

"No. Perhaps I should. But as long as we have the slightest doubt about him being who he says he is…"

"Agreed." She passed the key back to him. "Let's keep it to ourselves for now."

15

Satisfied there was no one hiding in the section they'd been given to search, Ben, Lorna and Rufus went back downstairs.

The others were already there. They had nothing to report either.

"At least we've established that there's no intruder in the house, which is some small comfort," Baldwin told them.

"What do we do now?" Ben asked.

"Providing you all agree, we should carry out that search of the grounds. And right away. This weather won't hold off much longer."

"If we're going to be tramping around outside," Felix said, "I'd feel happier if we had a way to communicate with each other. Rather than yelling, that is."

"There's probably something in the collection we

could use," Ben suggested. "Maybe a walkie-talkie set, or... Just a minute."

He went out of the sitting-room to a display cabinet in the hall. When he came back, he held aloft three silver whistles, attached to slender chains. "Old-fashioned police issue," he explained. "They're from some ancient Scotland Yard movie." He handed one to Baldwin.

"Good thinking," the Inspector said, turning to the others. "Each group will take a whistle. If you come across anybody give it a blast and the rest of us will find you. Again, let me stress that you shouldn't take any risks out there. We're dealing with a murderer, and retreat could be wiser than attack."

"Shall we keep to the same groups?" Crispin said.

"We may as well. Although, as we're going out of the house, it might be an idea to leave someone with Miss Stanislavovich and Belinda Whitbourne. As your group has four members, Mr Milhouse, I suggest one of you stays."

"The Reverend seems the best choice," Tyrone suggested.

Baldwin doesn't look too pleased with that, Ben noticed.

But the Inspector didn't object, only hesitated for a moment. "Very well," he muttered.

Avoiding the policeman's gaze, Kimball hurried off on his mission.

Once it was decided which area of the grounds each group would cover, they set off. Baldwin, Felix and Crispin, with the farthest portion of the estate to reach, went first. Tyrone, Helena and Parker left next. Ben, Lorna and Rufus brought up the rear.

Ben's group had been allotted the area behind the house, where extensive gardens eventually gave way to a small wood, then sloped down to a stream marking the estate's border.

The sky looked threatening. Light snow dusted the air, and would almost certainly be followed by a heavier fall. Trudging through the drifts proved hard going.

Before long they began to come across some of the statues littering Xanadu's grounds. Lorna spotted a larger-than-life effigy of John Wayne, one hand on a holstered gun, his wide-brimmed cowboy hat laden with snow.

Ben pointed out a massive black slab in the distance, startling against the whiteness. "I've no idea how Uncle Silvester came by it," he explained, "but that's the original monolith from *2001*."

Rufus was less than thrilled. He took a swig from his hip flask, then nodded towards a greenhouse and two sheds. "They look obvious places for someone to hide."

"Yeah," Ben agreed, "and to set an ambush. We should be careful checking them."

There was nothing suspicious in the greenhouse or first shed. But when they cautiously opened the second they found items that had nothing to do with gardening.

Scattered on the floor just inside was a heap of broken plastic. Lorna toed the debris. "Now we know what happened to Felix's mobile phone."

A mass of white sheeting lay beyond. Ben ventured in to examine it.

"It's Lawrence's air-bag," he reported, "and it's been repeatedly slashed. Looks like someone attacked it in a frenzy."

"It seems we've found the murderer's den," Rufus said.

"Or at least a place they found it convenient to dump stuff," Ben suggested. "It doesn't look as though anyone's actually been living here."

"Should we summon the others?" Lorna asked.

"I'd say not. This is an interesting discovery but not an emergency. We can tell them about it when we get back. Let's push on."

Soon, the house was out of sight, and trees were becoming more numerous.

"What the heck is *that*?" Lorna exclaimed. She pointed along the path they were walking. Something big and grey was half hidden by a frosty copse.

"Another statue," Ben told her. He smiled. "I remember it well from when I was a kid. Can you make out what it is?"

She shook her head.

"It's got its back to us, if that's a clue."

They kept walking. More of the thing came into view.

"Oh, *what*?" Lorna laughed, finally recognizing

the object they were approaching. "King Kong!"

"Yes," Ben confirmed. "Three or four times larger than a person. He's got his arms out in front of him, see? Beating his chest the way gorillas are supposed to. It's really well done."

"My brother certainly had eccentric tastes," Rufus commented.

"I think he had the most wonderful taste, Uncle Rufus. It was one of the reasons I loved coming here as a boy. You never knew what you were going to run into next."

The evidence in the shed was all that the search parties found. When everyone returned to the house their mood was one of relief and frustration.

"We should try to reach the outside," Rufus suggested, warming himself by the sitting-room fire. "Make up a party of two or three of the youngest and strongest." He sipped his brandy. Everyone else had settled on hot chocolate.

"Perhaps," Baldwin replied. "But it's damned risky under the circumstances. And in any event the weather's turning ugly again, and it's getting dark. We don't dare attempt it this evening."

"Another day wasted," Felix grumbled. "We're sitting ducks for this fruitcake. What do you propose doing about *that*, Inspector?"

"The only thing we can do, sir, is keep alert and hope my investigations lead us to the person responsible."

How very reassuring, Ben thought.

"How's Aunt Belinda, Inspector?" Lorna said.

"She's a little better actually. Hopefully she'll be taking dinner with us. But Miss Stanislavovich and the vicar could do with a break." He looked from Lorna to Ben. "How would you two like to relieve them for a while?"

"Sure," Lorna replied.

Ben nodded agreement.

"I'll come up with you," Baldwin added. "I need some papers from my room."

He told the others that Olga and Kimball would be down shortly. Then he led the way to the stairs.

Belinda's room was near Inspector Baldwin's. They came to his first.

"I'll see that someone looks in on you in about an hour," he promised, turning the handle of his bedroom door. "Keep your eyes and ears open."

They assured him they would and moved off. Walking to the end of the corridor, they turned sharp left and headed for a small flight of stairs.

But they didn't reach the first step.

There was a loud crash. It sounded like heavy furniture being toppled. Glass shattered. The commotion came from behind them.

Ben spun around and ran back towards Baldwin's room. Slower to react, it took Lorna a second to go after him. As they rounded the corner, they both heard a door slam.

First into Baldwin's corridor, Ben caught a brief

glimpse of someone at its far end. Whoever it was instantly vanished into gloom.

"Did you see that?" he said.

Lorna was jogging beside him now. "See what?"

"Never mind. Come on!"

Slamming into Baldwin's closed door, he battered it with his knuckles, calling the policeman's name.

There was only silence.

"For God's sake be careful," Lorna warned.

Ben grabbed the door handle.

16

Ben threw open the door.

Furniture had been scattered. Shards of glass from a broken mirror peppered the carpet. At first, he thought there was no one in the room, but then he heard a groan.

He found Baldwin on the floor on the far side of his bed, feebly attempting to rise. His eyes were glassy and unfocused. His face was deathly white.

Except for the trickles of scarlet running down from his hairline.

Ben knelt beside him. "Easy," he soothed, "easy. Don't try to move."

The Inspector slumped back with a pained sigh.

Lorna came to them. She produced a handkerchief and began gently dabbing at the blood. Baldwin winced. "Sorry," she apologized softly.

"What happened?" Ben asked.

Baldwin mumbled something, but they couldn't make sense of it.

Felix appeared at the door. "What the hell's going on?" he demanded. Crispin, Reverend Kimball and several of the others crowded behind him.

"The Inspector's been attacked," Lorna explained. "Looks like he was beaten about the head."

Ben noticed something under the bed. It was flat and black. He reached for it, careful to touch only the edges. What he eased into view was a movie clapper-board, as thick and heavy as a kitchen chopping block. There was blood on one end.

The wooden board had white stencilling which read *Scene – Take –*. And underneath, the title of the film: *The Hitman.*

"Here's the weapon," he told them. "Another example of the killer's warped sense of humour."

Felix leaned over the Inspector. "Who did this?" He mouthed the words slowly and clearly. "Who … was … it?"

Semi-conscious, Baldwin struggled to reply. At first, he was incoherent. Then he managed, "*Didn't … didn't see … who…*"

"All right, that's enough," Lorna decided, laying her hand on his brow. She looked up at the others. "Let's get him on to the bed, shall we?"

They carefully lifted Baldwin. He was laid with his head to one side so that Lorna and Olga could examine the wounds.

"These are quite nasty blows," Miss Stanislavovich

pronounced. "But unless there is internal damage I do not think they are *too* serious."

"He looks concussed," Rufus said.

"I'm sure he is," Lorna agreed. "And if that's the worst damage he's suffered, he's lucky."

Olga made for the door. "I will bring hot water and dressing."

"And I'd better get back to Belinda," Kimball decided.

"Neither of you should go alone," Ben cautioned.

Felix and Crispin exchanged nods. "We'll keep an eye on them," Felix announced as they hurried out.

And who's going to keep an eye on you? Ben thought. *Not being able to trust anyone is getting too complicated.*

He pushed that from his mind and returned his attention to Baldwin, who was breathing deeply with his eyes closed. "Think he'll be OK, Lorna?"

"I'm no medic, but with luck he could be. We'll have a better idea once we get the wound cleaned."

Apart from the comatose policeman, Tyrone, Helena and Rufus remained in the room with Ben and Lorna.

"You two got here quickly, didn't you?" There was a hint of accusation in the way Tyrone said it.

"What do you mean?" Ben retorted.

"Just what I say. You seem to have got here very quickly after the Inspector was attacked."

"If you recall," Lorna reminded him, "we left the sitting-room *with* Baldwin. We'd just gone our separate ways when we heard the uproar and ran back. Someone must have been hiding in here, waiting for him."

"The figure!" Ben exclaimed.

"What?" Lorna said.

"When we were running to get here I saw someone at the far end of the corridor. But it was so quick I couldn't tell who it was."

She nodded. "I remember you saying something."

"So it looks like our arrival might have interrupted Baldwin's attacker."

"Oh yeah?" Tyrone mocked. "You turn up at the scene of the crime and frighten off a mystery figure. Very convenient. But not the most original story I've heard."

Lorna's face darkened. "Are you saying what I think you're saying?"

"I'm just making the point that you two went off with the Inspector and the next thing we know he's been beaten half to death."

"If we were responsible then why didn't we finish the job?" Ben said. "We'd have to be stupid to leave Baldwin alive and run the risk of him exposing us."

"Perhaps you didn't have the chance to finish him," Helena put in. "We all got here pretty quickly."

"Neither you nor Lorna can *prove* where you were when Baldwin was attacked, Ben," Rufus added.

"Can the rest of you?" Ben countered. "Were you all together in the living-room before rushing up here?"

"Well ... no. We'd spread out a bit by then. But I'm sure nobody had the time to get to this floor and lay in wait."

"You don't know that for certain. The only ones with an alibi are Olga, Kimball and Aunt Belinda."

"Not really," Rufus informed him. "We ran into Miss Stanislavovich in the corridor outside, and she was coming from the bathroom. Although the Reverend was presumably still with Belinda."

"And she's under sedation," Ben reminded them. "So we have another incident which, in theory, any one of us could have been responsible for. And that's backed up by the fact that we've only just got through searching the house, so whoever it was I saw couldn't have been an intruder."

They were all mulling that over when Crispin and Olga returned. While she set about tending Baldwin's wounds, Ben and Lorna slipped out. Tyrone and Helena scowled at them as they left.

Once outside the room, Lorna whispered, "Assuming Baldwin's a real policeman, Ben, we may have just lost our only ally."

"Yeah, and managed to make ourselves suspects in the process."

The general consensus was that Inspector Baldwin would be likely to recover given time. But with both he and Belinda confined to bed, it seemed they might have to be put into the same room to make it easier to watch over them.

This problem was solved when Belinda insisted she was well enough to get up. As she was still recovering, it was decided that she and Kimball should take the first shift with Baldwin.

A couple of hours later, Ben and Lorna volunteered to relieve them. Tyrone grumbled in mild protest but only his daughter backed him. They all knew that, with everyone under suspicion, whoever went represented a risk. But they also realized that if anything happened to the policeman, they'd know who was to blame.

Ben and Lorna tapped on Baldwin's door and identified themselves before quietly entering.

Kimball and Belinda were in armchairs on either side of the bed. The Inspector, his eyes closed and head bandaged, was propped against a pile of pillows.

"How is he?" Lorna whispered.

"He seems to have calmed down," the vicar replied. "He's been resting peacefully for the last hour."

"And how are you, Aunt Belinda?" Ben added.

"Better than I was. Although I admit I'm ready for a change of scene." She looked to the priest. "Would you be kind enough to accompany me downstairs, Reverend?"

He took her arm and helped her from the room.

Ben advised them not to delay in joining the others before he closed and locked the door. Then he and Lorna occupied the chairs.

Almost immediately, Baldwin opened his eyes. He

ran his tongue over cracked lips and tried to talk. All he managed was a croak.

"Would you like a drink?" Lorna asked.

Baldwin slowly nodded, then briefly shut his eyes again, obviously pained at the effort. Lorna gently supported the back of his head with her hand as he sipped some water.

"*Better.*" He shifted slightly and blinked at them.

"Shall we call someone?" Ben said.

"*No. No … don't do that. I'm all … right, just … groggy. Need … to … tell you…*"

"Don't tire yourself," Lorna advised. "Whatever it is can wait."

"*Must … tell you … now.*" His breath was laboured.

"Take your time then," Ben urged him. "There's no rush."

"*Helpless … here. Taking chance … but … no choice. Have … to tell … someone.*"

"Tell us what?"

"*Be … wary … of … him.*"

Ben was confused. "Of who?"

"*Kimball. Shouldn't … trust … him.*"

"Why not?" He remembered how he and Lorna had speculated whether Kimball really was a priest, and added, "Is he an impostor?"

Baldwin managed a thin, fleeting smile. "*No. A … hypocrite!*"

"I don't understand. After all, the two of you arrived here together and—"

"*That was … because … he was … under arrest.*"

"*What?*" Lorna exclaimed.

"*On ... way to ... station ...to charge him. But ... weather...*"

"OK, we get the picture," Ben assured him. *Now we know why Baldwin treated Kimball so coldly*, he thought. "Can you tell us what you arrested him for?"

"*Blackmail.*"

"Blackmail?" Lorna repeated. "A man of the cloth?"

"*Won't be ... for ... much ... longer. Disgraced ... his ... position.*"

"Are you trying to tell us he's dangerous?" Ben asked. "That he could be the killer?"

"*Don't know. No ... record of ... violence. But ... be careful ... of him.*"

"We will."

"*Something ... else.*" Baldwin's voice was giving out. His eyes were becoming heavy-lidded. Lorna gave him a further sip of water.

"*Another ... person...*"

Ben leaned closer. "Yes? What other person?"

"*Not ... who they ... pretend to be. But ... can't ... can't ... remember... In ... back of ... mind ... I...*"

"Inspector? Inspector Baldwin?" Ben reached to shake him.

Lorna caught his hand. "Don't bother. He's well out. Let's leave him in peace for a while, shall we?"

He nodded glumly. "Of course. But I wish I knew what he was trying to tell us."

17

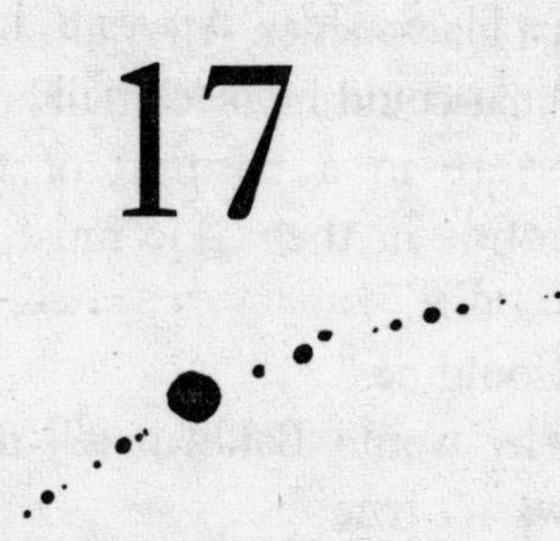

Lorna and Ben learnt no more from Baldwin that night. He was still sleeping soundly at around 11 p.m. when Felix and Rufus took over.

The hours of darkness passed without event.

Next morning, it was decided to move Baldwin down to the sitting-room, where they could keep an eye on him. Everyone also agreed to try spending as much time on the ground floor as possible and spread their forces less thinly.

Sitting in the hall's furthest corner, the most private place they could find, Ben and Lorna discussed what Baldwin had told them.

In hushed tones, Ben suggested, "I think we should keep what Baldwin said about Kimball to ourselves. Information is power, and we need any edge we can get in a situation like this."

"Agreed. But what if he told anyone else?"

"I doubt he did. He wasn't *that* out of it. And he did say it was us he'd chosen to tell, which implies it's our secret."

"But I've been wondering how plausible it is that Kimball's a blackmailer. After all, he's just a country parson. What could he blackmail anyone *about*?"

"Priests are in a position of trust, remember. People confide in them. He must hear all kinds of scandal and dirt."

"Hm. Could be."

"And why would Baldwin tell us something like that if it wasn't true?"

"Truth's a rare commodity in this place, Ben. Or hadn't you noticed? I can think of a couple of reasons Baldwin might have misled us."

"Such as?'

"First, he could simply have been delirious and talking rubbish. Understandably, after someone's just tried to cave in his head."

"Second?"

"We've never been entirely sure that Baldwin's who he says he is, if only because we have no real proof. Suppose he isn't a cop and was telling us a story to throw us off his trail."

"And he battered *himself* over the head, you mean?"

"Try to take this seriously. If he and Kimball are both fakes who've been conspiring together, and now they've fallen out, maybe Kimball was behind the attack."

"That's possible, but pointing a finger at his partner would be a high-risk strategy for Baldwin. It could push Kimball into spilling the beans."

Lorna sighed. "Nothing's easy, is it? Every time we think we've found a piece of the jigsaw it turns out not to fit. Have you given any thought to what else it was Baldwin wanted to tell us?"

"I've thought about it, yeah, but I haven't come up with anything. I'm hoping we can catch him alone again to ask."

"Why don't we try now?"

"Sure."

They wandered to the sitting-room. But too many of the others were coming and going for a private conversation with Baldwin. He was in a chair by the fire, wrapped in a thick blanket. His complexion was better, and his eyes brighter, although he was obviously still far from well.

Crispin sat by himself on the other side of the room, flipping through a dog-eared magazine. Rufus explored the drinks cabinet. Kimball and Belinda chatted quietly.

Felix was pacing the room, holding forth about the continuing bad weather. "This is ridiculous!" he complained. "Is it *ever* going to stop?"

His brother looked up. "Are *you*? Whingeing isn't going to make things better. Take it easy."

"Taking it easy isn't going to get us out of this fix, Crispin! I say we should try for help. Surely if two or three of us went—"

"That would leave too small a group to defend itself here," Crispin interrupted. "Not to mention how treacherous the conditions are outside, even for several people travelling together."

"And what if there's more than one murderer?" Rufus interjected. "We could end up in a situation where there's a killer in both the group going for help and with those remaining. It's too much of a chance."

Very sensible arguments, Ben decided. *But exactly what the murderer might say to persuade everyone to remain in the house.*

"Yes, it would be wisest to stay together," Kimball added. "If we allow ourselves to be divided we are more likely to be conquered."

Ben happened to glance at Baldwin. The policeman gave him a quick, conspiratorial wink. He took this as confirmation that what Baldwin had said about the vicar should be kept to themselves.

Then the Inspector spoke for the first time, in a voice still betraying his ordeal, but stronger than the night before. "I agree. We'd be mad to think about splitting ourselves in the present circumstances. My feeling is that if the weather were to take a dramatic turn for the better, then we should *all* leave the house to seek help. Until then, we sit tight."

Helena and Tyrone entered. "How are you, Inspector?" he asked.

"Mending, Mr Milhouse. And what have you been up to?"

"Daddy's just finished his meditation session,"

Helena answered for him. "He and Mommy used to meditate together every day at about this time. Didn't you, Pop?"

"Yeah, honey." He looked pained. "But talking about Mom's a little difficult for me right now."

As everyone settled down for small talk, Ben turned to Lorna and whispered, "I've got to do something. Would you stay here in case any of them tries to follow me, and delay them?"

She nodded, faintly enough that only he saw it.

"I'll see you in, say, ten minutes. In the study."

He got up and quietly left. No one seemed to take too much notice.

There was no one in the hall. He quickly made his way to the library. Then paused. There was a dead body inside, and it made him a little queasy to think about it.

Don't be an idiot, he chided himself, *this might be your only chance. Get in there!*

After one last look around he turned the handle and pushed open the door. The library was in darkness except for the weak light that penetrated the drawn curtains.

His eyes were drawn to Gwendoline's body. Somehow the white sheet covering it made the scene more ominous. He forced himself to concentrate on the job in hand. Fishing the key from his pocket, he inserted it in the lock. It was a perfect fit. Just to be sure, he turned it, confirming the match.

Returning the key to his jacket, he hastily exited.

There was still nobody about as he softly closed the door and went to the study. The lights were on. Someone, probably Olga, had set a fire in the hearth, making it a much more welcoming prospect than the death chamber he'd just left. As only a few minutes had passed, and Lorna hadn't arrived yet, he made himself comfortable in one of the over-stuffed desk chairs.

His eye was caught by a large book lying on a shelf just beyond his elbow. It had a colourful jacket, although he couldn't see the title. Out of idle curiosity, he reached over and took it.

He expected the weighty tome to be about some aspect of cinema, as the majority of Xanadu's books were. So he was surprised to find that it was called *The Universal Encyclopaedia of Plants*. He idly flipped through it. Then something caught his attention and he began reading. He hadn't quite finished when a soft knock sounded on the door.

Lorna came in. "Hi. Now, are you going to tell me what you've been up to?"

"I've established that the key I found fits the library."

"Good. Although I'm not sure where that gets us. What's that you're reading?"

"Oh, just something I found lying around." He showed it to her. "Not a movie book, unusually."

"Perhaps Uncle Silvester was trying to broaden his knowledge of gardening."

"Could be." He put the book down. "Anything

startling happening in the sitting-room?"

"Not really. More grumbling about the weather mostly, and a distinct lack of ideas about our predicament."

"Well, it is difficult knowing what to do next."

"Yeah, but there must be something better than hanging around here waiting for the thaw."

The door handle rattled. They turned, a little shaken at the unexpected interruption.

Olga came in. And stopped suddenly, taken aback at finding them there. "Oh! I am sorry if I have disturbed you."

"No, not at all, Miss Stanislavovich," Ben assured her. "We were just chatting." It crossed his mind that she might have been listening at the door. *She wouldn't have heard anything very interesting if she had*, he decided.

"What is that doing in here?" she asked, pointing to the encyclopaedia. "Did you bring it in?"

"Er, no," Ben said. "I found it here. Why?"

"It belongs in the library. Your uncle was very particular about there being a place for everything and everything being in its place. I am sure this was in the library the last time I saw it."

"You can't really put it back there now though, can you?" Lorna reminded her.

"No. No, of course. Not with that poor woman..." She shuddered. "But how ever did it come to be in here?" she repeated.

Ben was wondering about that too.

18

Everyone took lunch together. But before it finished Baldwin said he was going back to the sitting-room to rest. Seeing an opportunity to speak with the policeman privately, Ben and Lorna volunteered to accompany him.

Once settled, Ben wasted no time. "When you told us about Kimball, you were trying to remember something about another of the guests," he said. "Has it come to you yet?"

"Yes, it has. That blow to my head seems to have cleared some cobwebs. But it wasn't one of the guests I had in mind. It was Olga Stanislavovich."

"What about her?"

"I've been bothered about that woman ever since I got here. I knew I'd seen her somewhere before but I couldn't recall when or why. Then it came to me as I was lying upstairs. Seven or eight years ago I was sent to London for a spell with the Met and worked on a case concerning her. I wasn't directly involved, but I saw her on several occasions. Mostly in court."

"In court?" Lorna echoed.

"Yes. She was on trial for fraud. Got a two-year sentence, as I recall. The reason I couldn't place her before was that she wasn't calling herself by some fancy foreign name then. I knew her as Grace Andrews. She was from the East End of London and she had a string of convictions for obtaining money by false pretences. Using aliases was part of her *modus operandi*."

"I *knew* there was something odd about her accent!" Ben exclaimed. "Right from the start it seemed too ... theatrical, if you know what I mean."

Lorna nodded. "Yeah. As a matter of fact, it's her name that's been nagging at me. Stanislavovich is East European, possibly Polish, but it's almost always used as a first name. And here's the kicker, I think it's a name given to boys. It means 'son of'. I didn't mention it before because I wasn't entirely sure I was right."

"She's no more Polish than I am," Baldwin confirmed. "But I have to say that, like Kimball, there's no history of violence in her record. Or there wasn't then anyway. Which is not to say she isn't capable of it, of course."

"Exactly what kind of fraud was she engaged in?" Ben asked.

"That's what's interesting. Her speciality was

getting jobs with elderly, rich individuals and milking their bank accounts before disappearing. Forging cheques, that kind of thing."

"And now we find she's been working for rich, elderly Uncle Silvester," Lorna said. "Up to her old tricks, do you suppose, Inspector?"

"Seems a possibility, doesn't it? I certainly intend having your late uncle's accounts gone over thoroughly when we get out of here." He added as a grim afterthought, "*If* we get out of here."

"You know," Ben offered, "it's just possible that Silvester wasn't one of her victims. He could have known about her background. He had a reputation for taking in waifs and strays, and for giving people second chances. Look at Quentin Lawrence."

"Perhaps. But she's one of the heirs to this estate, remember. And I wonder if a woman with criminal tendencies could resist the temptation of trying to grab it all for herself. I've seen the prospect of a fortune turn too many people into murderers."

"What puzzles me, Inspector, is why you're confiding in us," Lorna said.

"Partly because I have to, to be honest. I'm not much use in my present state, and it struck me as wise to pass on any pertinent information I might have in case I don't come out of this. A sort of insurance policy. The other reason is less logical. When you've been a copper as long as I have you develop a kind of instinct about some people. It isn't always right, but I'm going to have to back it in this case."

"You don't think we're murder suspects, you mean?" Ben suggested.

"Well, let's just say I think of you two as being *less* suspect than everybody else. No offence."

Ben grinned. "None taken. And for what it's worth, your instinct hasn't let you down this time."

"I'd like to believe that, son," Baldwin replied.

"What should we do with this information about Olga?" Lorna wanted to know. "Or do I mean Grace?"

"File it in your minds and kept it to yourselves," the Inspector told them. "I don't think she's recognized me. It was some years ago, after all. My feeling is that there's no point in confronting her with any of this at the moment. And we should stick to calling her Olga, for obvious reasons."

Before he could say anything else the sitting-room door flew open.

Talk of the devil, Ben thought.

"There has been an act of vandalism!" the phoney Olga exclaimed.

"What do you mean?" Baldwin demanded.

"It is quite silly … senseless. In the kitchen!"

"I'll go," Ben offered. "Lorna, you stay here with the Inspector." He trotted after the departing housekeeper.

Ben couldn't see what the fuss was about when they arrived in the kitchen.

"There!" she said, pointing to a solid oak table against the far wall.

He went over to investigate. There were five framed pictures on the wall. Closer examination showed that they weren't pictures as such; each was an arrangement of dried flowers. A sixth picture had been removed and was now empty and shattered on the table top.

Frowning, he turned to Olga. "Let's get this straight. You're saying that someone came in here, took down a framed display of dried flowers, smashed it and stole them?"

"Yes! It is mad. Why would anyone want to do such a thing?"

Irritatingly, she pronounced "thing" as *zing*. He wanted to tell her to stop the play-acting, to let her know he knew her secret. But he bit back the impulse.

"Are these valuable in any way?" he asked, nodding at the pictures.

"I am sure not. In fact, they are quite new. Mr Silvester had them mounted here just a few weeks ago. They are flowers from Xanadu's gardens. But valuable? No."

"Do you have any idea which particular plant this frame contained?"

"Only Lawrence would have known that. I am ignorant of such things. I do recall they had dark green leaves and small white berries. But that is probably of little help to you."

Probably of no help whatsoever, he reflected as he left her sweeping the glass up with a dustpan and brush. *Why the* heck *would anyone want to steal something like that?*

Lorna and Baldwin could offer no explanation for the theft either.

But the new mystery wasn't foremost in Ben's mind. Other possibilities were forming on the edge of his consciousness. Fantastic possibilities.

As soon as they could, he and Lorna made for their private corner in the hall.

"I'm starting to get a vague idea of what might be going on here," he revealed.

"Brilliant, Ben! Well, don't just sit there, *tell* me!"

"I can't. Not at the moment. I've got some checking to do, and quite a bit more thinking."

"Oh, come on! Can't you at least give me a hint?"

"To be frank, there are two reasons why I don't want to tell you anything yet. First, my theory's pretty bizarre. If it proves to be wrong, I'm going to look the biggest fool in creation."

"You wouldn't to me."

"Thanks." He smiled. "The second reason is that I don't want to put you in danger by saying too much. Information is power, remember? And if who I think is responsible for the murders gets so much as an inkling that I've shared my thoughts with you... Well, your life's on the line."

"It is anyway, Ben. We're all on this lunatic's list already, remember?"

"I'd rather your name didn't go to the top of it.

Just bear with me for now, will you?"

Reluctantly, she nodded.

"But there is a way you can help. I said I had to check something. It'd be really useful if you could cover for me when I do it."

"Sure. When?"

"As soon as there's a chance of slipping away from the others unnoticed. Stay with me and be ready."

"OK. But if there's any risk involved you will be careful, won't you, Ben?"

"You bet. Shall we go back now?"

When they entered the living-room, they found everyone present and engaged in a lively discussion.

"Ah, there you are," Rufus greeted them, a glass in his hand as usual. "Tyrone here has suggested a little entertainment."

"I hope it's nothing like the last time he tried entertaining us," Ben remarked, remembering Lawrence's fatal stunt.

Tyrone heard him. "This is guaranteed safe," he promised, holding up a handful of videos. "My last couple of movies, one of which hasn't been released in this country yet. I thought a première might fill a couple of hours and take our minds off things."

For want of any better idea, everyone agreed to give it a try, although some agreed more readily than others. In particular, Belinda was concerned that the movies might be too violent for her present state of nerves.

"Don't worry about that, honey," Tyrone assured her, "we'll leave out the heavier stuff."

They all began filing out, Baldwin steadied by Felix and Crispin.

Ben and Lorna held back. "This is the chance I need," he whispered. "Go with them and make an excuse for me if necessary. I'll join you as quickly as I can."

As soon as they were out of sight he tore upstairs. When he reached the room he wanted it crossed his mind it might be locked. But he was in luck. Its occupant hadn't bothered. After searching for a few minutes, he found a brown attaché case on top of the wardrobe. When he placed it on the bed and opened it his suspicions were confirmed. Carefully, he put it back.

Then he dashed down to the basement at breakneck speed. It seemed no one had noticed his absence. Taking a seat next to Lorna, at the rear of the small auditorium, he panted, "Mission accomplished." She squeezed his hand and gave him a secret smile.

Once Olga, Kimball and Rufus had finished laying out a table with coffee, tea and snacks, the show commenced.

Unfortunately, the first video turned out to be Helena's show reel, an hour long movie designed to display her talents for casting directors and producers. Ben felt they'd been lured down there under false pretences if this was the level of "entertainment" on offer. But eventually the demonstration of Helena's inept tap-dancing, atrocious acting and dire singing came to an end.

Amid the thin, ragged applause, Lorna whispered, "That was at least fifty-nine minutes too long."

Then one of Tyrone's feature films came on. It was a crime caper, filled with tedious car chases and predictable shoot-outs between actors hewn from solid wood. The best Ben could say was that it passed some time.

When it finished, Tyrone began running another of his epics, a horror movie with a particularly gruesome opening. But his audience decided to quit while they were still ahead. The only exception was Crispin. He went to the refreshments table.

"Are you coming, Crispin?" Felix called.

"Thought I might watch a bit of this," he said, nodding at the screen. "I'd welcome a few minutes away from other people, to be honest." He dropped into a seat and began sipping his coffee.

Felix was a little doubtful. "Well, OK. But don't be long, right?"

"Sure."

His brother went to catch up with the others.

It was twenty minutes later, upstairs in the sitting-room, before they realized Crispin hadn't joined them.

"Your brother's taking his time, isn't he, Felix?" Rufus said.

The group exchanged anxious glances.

"It might be an idea to check on him," Baldwin suggested.

They all started for the door, the younger and fitter running ahead. Felix, Ben and Lorna clattered down the stairs and arrived at the cinema together. Inside, the lights were still dimmed and Tyrone's film continued to run. Crispin sat in the front row.

"Come on, Crispin!" Felix yelled. "You must have had enough by now!"

There was no reply.

The others were crowding into the room. Felix walked up the aisle. The movie soundtrack boomed with raucous music and shrill sound effects.

"OK, Crispin, your time's up," he said. "Let's go."

Crispin maintained his silence, apparently engrossed by the spectacle on the screen. Felix went over and shook his arm.

His brother toppled to one side. Lifeless.

Belinda screamed. The other guests rushed to investigate. They cleared a path for Baldwin, whose slower movements had kept him back. He took Crispin's wrist and held it.

"He's dead."

"No!" Felix cried. "He *can't* be!"

"I can assure you he is, sir. I'm sorry."

In the hubbub that followed, Ben noticed a cup at the corpse's feet. It still contained a small quantity of brown liquid. He gingerly lifted it and sniffed, detecting a sweet, slightly fruity smell that had nothing to do with coffee.

"Maybe it was the movie," Helena blurted. "Dad's films are scary. Crispin could have died of shock!"

"*Stupid* girl!" Lorna exclaimed. "People don't die of shock watching lousy horror movies."

"Don't you call my Dad's movies—"

"Please!" Baldwin snapped. "Let's be calm, shall we? Squabbling doesn't help." He turned to Felix. "Did your brother have any kind of heart condition?"

"What?" He dragged his eyes from the body of his sibling. "No. No, of course not! He was incredibly fit."

Ben placed a hand on Baldwin's arm and the policeman allowed himself to be led a few steps away from the chaos of arguments, accusations and weeping. He showed the Inspector the cup. "I'm sure we'll find the reason for Crispin's death here," he whispered.

"Poison?"

"Something like. I might even be able to tell you what it is."

Baldwin raised an eyebrow at him.

"I'll explain later. And I think I can explain more than that. I reckon I now know what this nightmare's all about. And who's responsible."

19

Ben and the Inspector were alone in Baldwin's room.

"I'm taking an awful lot on trust here," the policeman said.

"I know. But now I've explained my theory, can you think of a better way to flush out the killer?"

"Assuming you're right, no. I'm not sure I buy your explanation, though. You have to admit it's a little ... *fantastic*."

"Yes, and there's always the chance that I'm wrong. That's why we have to stage it the way I'm suggesting."

Baldwin sighed. "All right, I agree. But only because these are such unusual circumstances, mind."

"Thanks, Inspector," Ben smiled. "I'm sure it'll work out if we stick to the script."

Baldwin indicated a pile of books and papers on

his bedside table. "This lot might be of interest to you, by the way."

"What is it?"

"Proof that I haven't been idle. Those are the accounts for Silvester Whitbourne's estate. Remember I said I'd check them out when we were talking about the woman calling herself Olga?"

"Yeah."

"Well, I discovered that she didn't have access to these main accounts or large amounts of cash. Only a small household budget."

"Where did you get the books then?"

"I did a bit of nosing around in the study earlier and found them with some other items belonging to Parker."

"Parker? Surely it's not a lawyer's job to work out somebody's accounts?"

"No, it isn't. But it seems your uncle let him deal with the accountancy firm on his behalf. It's not an unusual arrangement, particularly when a client has no reason to distrust his solicitor."

"And?"

"Well, I'm no accountant, but I've been a copper long enough to recognize fiddled books when I see them."

"There are irregularities?"

"That's a polite way of putting it, Ben. Money's gone missing without adequate explanation. Not a great deal, but enough to make me suspicious."

"Just a minute, Inspector. Uncle Silvester was a

businessman, and a very successful one. He'd spot fiddled account books right away."

"Yes. But as I said, he had no reason to doubt Parker's word. He probably didn't bother to check."

"It would fit in with his character. My parents always said he was too trusting."

"The other possibility," Baldwin added, "is that the books have been altered since his death."

"The people in this place seem to have no end of secrets."

"Or motives. Shall we get on with your little drama now?"

Baldwin didn't explain why he wanted everyone to gather in the cinema, just insisted that they do it. There was a certain amount of low-level grumbling when he and Ben appeared after letting them stew for twenty minutes.

They were all seated in the front rows. Ben and the Inspector stood in front of them. Without preamble, Baldwin began. "We're here because I believe we can get to the bottom of the events that have taken place by going through certain facts that have come to light. And we'll do it in a way that some of you might consider a little unusual. I'm going to leave most of the talking to Ben. He has my full co-operation and backing to assist in this part of the investigation."

"What *is* this, Inspector?" Tyrone demanded. "The boy's as much a suspect as anyone else. How come he's doing your dirty work now?"

"If you'll be patient, Mr Milhouse, I think everything will become clear. Carry on, please, Ben."

For better or worse, here we go! Ben told himself.

"Let me start by saying that, as you must all realize, every one of Silvester Whitbourne's heirs stands to greatly gain from the death of the others. We're talking about a unique collection, a house and land which together are worth millions. I think my uncle was wrong to draft his will the way he did, because it created the situation we find ourselves in now. But his error was based on the assumption that people would behave decently, so he isn't to be criticized for that. As a matter of fact, we now know that he realized he'd made a mistake and tried to put it right. But more on that later."

Several voices were raised, demanding he explain.

"As Ben said," Baldwin told them, "we'll return to that aspect later. Now let him get on with it."

They quietened down. Ben cleared his throat. "I want to run through all of you individually, in order to point out the range of motives we're presented with here. If I offend any of you, well, that's too bad. Hurt feelings shouldn't matter in the face of a string of murders." He paused. "Let's begin with you, Uncle Rufus. It's common knowledge in the family that you had to leave the country some years ago after a scandal. As I understand it, you were suspected of selling shares in a non-existent gold mine."

"I was never charged!" Rufus objected.

"Perhaps not. But you have to admit that a cloud

of suspicion has hung over you ever since. I'd guess that you didn't change your ways in Australia, and that you could use cash to disentangle yourself from whatever your present problem is."

Rufus tried to speak again, but Baldwin silenced him.

Ben turned to Milhouse. "As for you, Uncle Tyrone, your last few movies have been expensive flops. No doubt you could use money to bolster your waning fortunes. Not to mention paying all the bills you daughter's running up in her quest to be a star."

Ben addressed her next. "You're very ambitious, Helena Belle, and it's not impossible that you'd try to obtain the wealth you crave through murder. I've certainly seen indications that you could be ruthless enough."

"Are you going to let him talk to me like this, Daddy?" she whined, rising from her seat. "How could anyone think I'd kill my own Mom?"

"Yeah!" Tyrone raged, leaping up too. "Where the hell do you get off—"

"*That's enough!*" Baldwin warned them.

The Milhouses shut up and sat down.

Ben continued. "You, Felix, would have made a great deal of money out of solely controlling the inheritance. And you tried to keep the proposed theme park a secret from the rest of us."

"Are you saying I killed my own brother?"

"The two of you didn't always get on, we all saw

that, and he voted against you over selling the collection. Something you obviously weren't expecting. And I could speculate about the fact that Crispin sat on the council's planning committee. Perhaps you were relying on him to push through a planning application to refurbish Xanadu, and he broke the agreement."

"Speculate as much as much as you like! That's a slur on my brother and me, and I resent it!"

"Your protest is noted," Baldwin said coolly.

It was Belinda Whitbourne's turn. "It seems Uncle Jeremy defrauded some of his clients, Aunt Belinda," Ben stated.

"That was never proved!"

"Just because it didn't go to court doesn't mean there was no substance to the allegations," Baldwin informed her.

"You might have wanted money to pay back those clients," Ben continued. "Then again, it's well known that you have an expensive lifestyle, way beyond your late husband's means. Silvester's fortune would have solved several problems for you."

"This is outrageous!"

He ignored her. "And now those of you who aren't family members. First, Miss Olga Stanislavovich. Or should I say Grace Andrews?"

She was taken aback for a second, then said, "Grace Andrews? I do not know what you are talking about!"

"You can drop the fancy lingo, Grace," the

Inspector interjected. "I know who you are and I've seen you in court. You can't talk your way out of it."

"*Damnation!*" she spat, her fake foreign accent forgotten. "But you're not nailing me for these murders." Under other circumstances Ben might have laughed at how quickly the broad London intonation replaced the false East European one. "Silvester knew all about my past," she went on. "He was giving me a fresh start. I swear I wasn't abusing his trust."

Ben left her to her embarrassment and addressed Dominic Parker. "And we know that you have been misappropriating the estate's money."

"That's a filthy lie!" the lawyer blustered. "How dare you make such—"

"I think you'll find the Inspector has enough proof to bring charges," Ben interrupted.

Parker turned ashen as Baldwin nodded.

"As I understand it, you fortunately hadn't got away with too much," Ben continued. "But the prospect of seeing the estate passing into the hands of twelve other people and beyond your ability to milk it further might have pushed you to desperate measures. I imagine that in the event of none of the heirs surviving you would have continued acting on the estate's behalf."

Parker's uncomfortable silence confirmed Ben's last assumption. He turned his attention to Kimball. "Finally we come to you, Reverend. Although from what I've heard you don't deserve the title. I now know that you were under arrest when you arrived here with the Inspector, and that he was taking you in to be charged with blackmail."

"I'm innocent!"

"It remains for a court of law to decide that," Baldwin reminded him.

"Somewhere along the line you've allowed yourself to become corrupted," Ben added. "As a matter of fact, I'm sure that Lorna and I actually witnessed you in the act of trying to find something incriminating on someone. I'm referring to when we came across you in my uncle's office. Who was the victim this time, Reverend?"

The woman they had thought of as Olga spoke up. "It was probably me! I was already being blackmailed by this man. He found out about my past, perhaps on one of those occasions when he came here to see Mr Silvester. My late employer had a full record of all my past misdeeds. He even had newspaper clippings of my trial." She jerked a thumb in Kimball's direction. "He was always nosing around, and no doubt discovered this. If my criminal record was known I'd be ruined in this community. It would have put an end to my hopes of starting a new life."

"You're a fool, Kimball," the Inspector added. "You couldn't resist your old ways even when you were under arrest, could you? No wonder it wasn't too hard catching you in the first place."

Kimball visibly shrank in his chair.

"Well," Ben concluded. "As you can see, everyone

had motives of some kind to—"

"Everyone except you and her, it seems!" Felix shouted, pointing at Lorna. "Don't tell me neither of you is attracted by immense wealth!"

"If you have any accusations to make about Ben Whitbourne or Lorna Ferguson, kindly make them now," Baldwin stated. "Otherwise hold your peace."

Felix lapsed into surly silence.

"Now what was that about Silvester knowing he'd made a mistake?" Rufus asked.

Several of the others supported him.

"I was just coming to that," Ben told them. "When the Inspector and I were going through my uncle's effects, we came across this." He reached into his jacket pocket and took out a videotape in a plain box. Holding it up for them all to see, he explained, "From some scribbled notes we found with it, we have reason to believe that this is a *second* will, made just before he died. So soon before his death, in fact, that he didn't have time to tell Mr Parker about it."

"What does it say?" Milhouse wanted to know. He wasn't alone. The question was on everyone's lips.

Ben waved them into silence. "We think it differs substantially from the one we saw. In essence, it seems to say that there was only *one* heir to Silvester's fortune."

There were gasps and exclamations.

"And we believe there's a stipulation that if this person were to die, the inheritance couldn't be passed on to any of their relatives. It looks as though, in the event of this heir's death, the entire estate was to go to a charitable trust in which the family has no stake whatsoever."

"Just a minute," Felix said. "You keep using expressions like you 'think', you 'believe' and 'it seems'. Don't you *know*?"

"The fact is that I'm basing all I've said on the few notes we found. We haven't looked at the tape yet."

"Why not?"

"For some reason, Uncle Silvester chose to record this new will with a Beta system camera, not the much more widely used VHS system most of us are familiar with. Perhaps he did it as a security precaution. And he doesn't seem to have made any VHS copies. Or copies of any kind, come to that. This is the only one. In any event we haven't been able to find a Beta system video recorder in the house to play it on."

"So this is all supposition!" Rufus exclaimed, almost gleefully. "You don't actually *know* what's on that tape at all, do you?"

"No," Ben admitted. "But we're about to find out. I've enough technical knowledge to convert the video projector right here in the cinema so that it can play this tape."

"And apparently it's going to take Ben about an hour to make the adjustments," Baldwin announced. "So I suggest we leave him in peace to get on with it. Let's go and have a drink or something and come back when he's ready for the screening."

There were complaints about the delay, but Baldwin firmly ushered everyone out.

Left alone, Ben made his way up to the projection booth and waited. He didn't even bother taking the video out of his pocket. There was no point.

Sitting in silence, he started to feel apprehensive about the plan. Maybe it wouldn't go the way he anticipated. He was just as afraid that it would.

About fifteen minutes passed. He was starting to think that his theory could be wrong, when suddenly there was a tremendous crash. The door flew open, and someone rushed into the room.

Everything happened too quickly after that. The figure was bearing down on him. In the glow of the overhead light a knife flashed.

He threw himself at his attacker, grabbing their hand and trying to stop the blade reaching his face. Their struggle took them across the room. Cans of film and stacks of videos were dashed to the floor. A chair overturned with a loud impact.

Then he was aware of others in the room. They piled into his assailant, snatching away the knife. Eventually their captive was still, restrained by Baldwin's handcuffs and held by several pairs of arms.

The mist of terror cleared from his eyes, the adrenalin pumped less furiously, and Ben looked into the face of the murderer.

It was exactly who he expected. But he still couldn't suppress the shudder that ran up his spine.

20

Gwendoline Whitbourne regarded Ben with pure hatred.

He couldn't get over the thought that he was staring into the eyes of a dead person.

"Take her away!" Baldwin snapped.

Felix and Rufus dragged off their struggling, cursing prisoner. They passed Lorna at the projection room's door. She flattened herself against the wall to let them through, slack-jawed at the sight.

Then she hurried to Ben. "Are you all right?" she asked anxiously.

"Fine," he smiled.

"Gwendoline will be locked in a spare bedroom," Baldwin explained, "one without a window."

"What happened about Tyrone?" Ben said.

"He did exactly what you said he would. At the first opportunity he slunk off. To tell his wife what had happened, of course."

"And to arrange to have me killed and the video spirited away."

"They couldn't afford to have a later will that cut everyone out. And as they thought it was the only copy, they had to seize the opportunity of destroying it."

"I'm glad they jumped the way we predicted they would."

"You can say that again. Anyway," Baldwin continued, "while Milhouse was away, I explained the situation to everyone else. They took some convincing, I can tell you. But I managed it, and when he came back I arrested him. He's cuffed in his room at the moment."

"And Helena?"

"She's with Belinda upstairs. I'm sure you're right about her not being involved."

"This is all very interesting," Lorna fumed, "but will somebody *please* explain about Gwendoline? For God's sake, she's ... she was ... *dead*!"

Ben grinned. "Why don't we go down to the viewing theatre and I'll fill you in on the details?"

Baldwin joined them on the plush seats of the cinema's first row.

"Now tell me!" Lorna demanded impatiently. "And I want it *all*, right from the beginning."

"OK," Ben said. "Tyrone Milhouse is in serious financial difficulties. As it turns out, so is Gwen. Her health club's apparently running at a massive loss. They arrived here hoping the will would bail them out. But Tyrone got impatient waiting for it to be read and broke into the desk in the study. As soon as they realized the will's implications, they conceived their plan. And considering they had to do it so quickly, it was a brilliant scheme. Of course, having everyone isolated here by the weather gave them an opportunity that probably wouldn't come again."

Lorna was beginning to recover from the shock. "And presumably the first stage was to cut the phone lines and immobilize the cars," she offered.

"Right. But the really clever bit was faking Gwen's murder."

"Yes, how the heck did they *do* that, Ben?"

"There were two clues that led me to figuring it out: the fact that Aunt Gwendoline meditated, and Uncle Tyrone's expertise with make-up. Remember him telling us he'd worked in a Hollywood studio's make-up department for several years?"

"Yeah. But I don't see what any of that has to do with faking a murder."

"It went like this. On our first night here, when Tyrone and Gwen were supposed to be up in their room after dinner, they actually sneaked down to the library. He applied make-up to her that looked like a fatal head wound. Then he left, and joined us. At that point, I believe things went wrong for them. She should have locked the door, fired the shotgun out of the open window, into the air, closed the window again and played dead. But she forgot to lock the door *first*. Hearing us running to the library, she panicked, hurriedly secured the door and flung the key out of the open French windows, which she had no time to close. She probably counted on retrieving it later, or getting Tyrone to. The original plan must have been to hide the key somewhere in the room, somewhere clever enough it couldn't be easily found, but she had no time for that either."

"And they needed the key so she could get in and out of the room when she needed to."

"Exactly."

"Why didn't she just hide it in her clothes?"

"She was wearing a nightgown, remember? No pockets."

"And that stain on the key?"

"I finally remembered what it was. It's a cosmetic preparation they use in the movies to simulate blood. It eventually goes gummy and turns a dark colour. She must have got some on the key when she handled it. I confirmed that Tyrone had a supply of the stuff when I found his make-up case in their room."

"How does meditation come into it?"

"I recalled reading that people who have a lot of experience with meditation and yoga, like Gwen, can put themselves into a trance state that slows down their pulse and heartbeat. Had Felix kept his hand on her wrist a little longer than he did, she would have been exposed. It was one of several calculated risks they took. Another was that we wouldn't try to move the body."

"Or search it for the key?"

"Yes. But I think anybody capable of slowing down their heartbeat and pulse would be able to play dead long enough for the short time that would have taken. It was later, when Inspector Baldwin turned up unexpectedly, that they were really lucky. Gwen was fortunate to be in the library when he and I went in, and obviously had just enough time to pose as a corpse again. Even so, she must have been terrified that the Inspector would examine her closely. Apart from anything else, she would have been *warm*, no matter how good an act she put on."

"I was at fault there," Baldwin admitted. He looked embarrassed. "But I was totally fooled by that make-up job, and Ben told me that Felix had checked for signs of life when Gwen was first found. And, dammit it, you just don't expect a corpse to be anything other than dead!"

"I wouldn't be too hard on yourself," Ben said. "The genius of Gwen and Tyrone's plan was precisely that people see what they *expect* to see."

"Yes, like employing the principle that one of the best ways to hide something is to leave it in plain sight," the Inspector commented. "I see that now. I should have seen it *then*."

"It was a perfectly ingenious idea," Lorna remarked. "What better alibi than being thought dead?"

"Yes," Ben agreed. "It gave Gwen complete freedom of movement and an ideal cover for committing the murders, with some help from Tyrone when he could manage it."

"So she was the figure you saw in the basement, and again near the Inspector's room?"

"That's right. She activated the model shark that killed Jeremy. And if it hadn't been for our arrival, she would have battered the Inspector here to death. I think the attempt on his life, incidentally, was motivated by the fact that he was an irritant to their scheme."

"And Quentin Lawrence?"

"My hunch there is that he guessed the truth somehow and was clumsily trying to blackmail Tyrone into giving him a part in his next picture. Killing him served two purposes: shutting him up and further increasing the Milhouses' share of the inheritance."

"So it was Gwen who removed the air-bag?"

"She had at least an hour to do it. Maybe Tyrone was able to slip out for a few minutes to help her."

"That leaves Crispin."

"Actually, it was his murder that provided the final clue. I've a feeling that the pathology report on him will show he was poisoned by seeds from a Lily of the Valley plant. Those seeds were taken from the framed display of dried flowers stolen from the kitchen. Those displays weren't very old and the berries still retained their potency. Tyrone dropped the crushed seeds into Crispin's cup as he left the cinema."

"So it was the *book* that put it all together for you."

"Yes. I didn't know Lily of the Valley was poisonous until I read about it in the encyclopaedia. And I only looked at that part of the book because a small piece of blank paper fell from the page. I figured somebody was especially interested in that entry and got careless. What got me putting two and two together was when Olga, or Grace rather, told us that the book belonged in the library. I knew nobody would have gone in there to take out a book, not with a supposedly dead body on the floor, so there had to be a less than innocent explanation."

"They really did take some chances, didn't they?" Lorna remarked. "I mean, what about the time you went to check that the key fitted the library lock? Gwen might not have been there. Or up and about in the room."

"Which would have given both of us a nasty shock! And something else that was significant, but only occurred to me afterwards, was when we were searching the house and Tyrone insisted on checking the library alone."

"That must have been an anxious moment for him."

"You bet! But they were right in thinking that none of us would even consider the possibility of suspecting a person we thought was dead. It was good psychology."

"I don't understand how they hoped to get away with so many murders."

"At first, the plan was to kill only those of us who voted against selling the collection," Ben explained, "and to make the murders look like accidents. Jeremy's death, for example, could have been seen as an unfortunate mishap. Of course they soon realized they'd be unlikely to get away with that. Thinking they *could* was the flaw in their original plan, no doubt because they conceived it so quickly. But they'd already committed one murder, and were in too deep to stop. So they came up with another scheme."

"Which was?"

"To kill all of us. Then, rather than trying to claim the inheritance, they would have stripped the collection of some of its choicest items and disappeared. As you said yourself, Lorna, there are individual pieces here worth a fortune. With his connections in the film world, Tyrone could have sold them to wealthy collectors on the black market."

"Now he knows the game's up," Baldwin added, "he's coming clean on the whole thing. They'd planned to abandon their life in the States and run away from the debts. They had fake passports under new identities. Those would have been used to escape from here. They might even have torched the house to cover their tracks."

"What about Helena?" Lorna asked. "Would they have taken her?"

"It doesn't look like it."

"Wow. And they could have got away with it. It

was fortunate you two came across Uncle Silvester's new will. It proved the perfect bait for luring Gwen out."

Ben and the policeman burst into laughter.

Lorna was puzzled. "What is it? What have I said?"

"All that stuff about a second will was moonfluff," Ben told her. "We made it up and hoped they'd swallow the story."

He reached into his pocket, brought out the video and handed it to her. She opened the unmarked case and looked inside.

The tape had a label reading *The Best of the Three Stooges*.

"My turn! My turn!" Lorna clamoured.

Ben handed her one of the long red cylinders. "Hold it at arm's length and point it straight up," he instructed. "Now pull hard on that piece of string on the side."

The rescue flare belched a gout of flame and shot its exploding payload far into the air. It detonated in a huge orange explosion far over Xanadu's grounds.

"This was a great idea, Ben."

"Thanks. It occurred to me there might be something in the collection we could use to attract attention. These flares came from a movie about the Titanic. I think Silvester would understand our using them, under the circumstances. Wish I'd thought of it earlier though."

"Talking of your uncle," Baldwin said, handing them each a glass of champagne, "let's drink to him."

"Here's to Uncle Silvester," Ben proposed, clinking his glass against Lorna's, "and his collection."

"Aren't you joining us, Helena Belle?" Lorna asked.

The would-be starlet looked over and shook her head. "No. Bad for the complexion. I'm going back in, the weather's not that much better. Anyway, I've got things to think about."

"Right," Ben said sympathetically. "You're worried about your mum and dad, naturally."

"Of course," she pouted. "I mean, what do you think all this is going to do to my *image*?"